THE RESTRICTIONS OF CORA

Kristie Price

Copyright © 2023 Kristie Price

All rights reserved

The characters and events portrayed in this book are fictitious. Any similarity to real persons, living or dead, is coincidental and not intended by the author.

No part of this book may be reproduced, or stored in a retrieval system, or transmitted in any form or by any means, electronic, mechanical, photocopying, recording, or otherwise, without express written permission of the publisher.

This novel contains topics regarding alcohol, domestic disputes/divorce, and sex. The Restrictions of Cora is intended for readers 18 years of age or older.

ISBN: 9798385895038

Cover design: Ashley Santoro
Editor: Mariel Bard

To the quiet girls - who silently fight their battles and bend until they finally break. This is your sign to take your life back for you. It's your time now.

*"Real love doesn't meet you at your best.
It meets you in your mess."*

- J.S. PARK

CONTENTS

Title Page
Copyright
Dedication
Epigraph
Playlist

CHAPTER ONE	1
CHAPTER TWO	9
CHAPTER THREE	23
CHAPTER FOUR	32
CHAPTER FIVE	44
CHAPTER SIX	60
CHAPTER SEVEN	72
CHAPTER EIGHT	85
CHAPTER NINE	104
CHAPTER TEN	116
CHAPTER ELEVEN	127
CHAPTER TWELVE	141
CHAPTER THIRTEEN	154
CHAPTER FOURTEEN	165
CHAPTER FIFTEEN	176
CHAPTER SIXTEEN	187
CHAPTER SEVENTEEN	194
CHAPTER EIGHTEEN	207

CHAPTER NINETEEN	219
CHAPTER TWENTY	229
Jeremiah's Song to Cora	243
About The Author	245

PLAYLIST

First Date - blink-182
I'm Lost Without You - blink-182
Your House - Jimmy Eat World
Alcohol and Alter Boys - Bayside
Megan - Bayside
The Story So Far - New Found Glory
Sucker - New Found Glory
Have Faith in Me - A Day to Remember
Calm Before the Storm - Fall Out Boy
A Little Less Sixteen Candles, A Little More "Touch Me" - Fall Out Boy
Terrible Things - Mayday Parade
Everything Sucks - Reel Big Fish
Growing Up - McFly
Sunday Morning - No Doubt
In This Diary - The Ataris
All That I've Got - The Used
This Photograph is Proof (I Know You Know) - Taking Back Sunday
Island (Float Away) - The Starting Line
Every Thug Needs a Lady (Acoustic) - Alkaline Trio
She's Automatic - Rancid
Bad Luck - Social Distortion
Last Hope - Paramore
My Heart - Paramore

CHAPTER ONE

Don't

August 2005

The sun is peeking through the trees in my backyard, hitting my face and heating my cheeks. I feel like I'm being wrapped in a warm hug, and I embrace it, letting it comfort me as I gently swing back and forth in a hammock on this sweltering day in Portland, Maine. I'm trying to forget that this is the last week of summer vacation. But it's hard to ignore that my senior year of high school starts next week. I'm annoyed to be going back to school but also . . . relieved.

I have two reasons for being simultaneously relieved and annoyed. Reason number one: I hate high school. Especially Rock Point High. I have never felt like I fit in, and because of that, I don't have many friends. I'm labeled by my classmates as being different—and not in a good way. I would call myself unique, sure, but truth be told, I'm actually a pretty normal girl. I enjoy spending my weekends seeing local pop/punk and emo bands. I love wearing black, and the bright-red streaks in my hair are what I would consider one of my best assets. Okay, so I *am* different, but honestly, I feel like every other teenager just trying to make it through high school.

For the past few days, I've been reminding myself that it's just one more year and then I am finally free.

Moving on to reason number two: My parents have recently filed for divorce since they haven't been getting along for about two years, ever since my dad lost his job. In that time, I have spent countless nights overhearing screaming matches and the sounds of plates and cups being thrown across the kitchen and smashing to the floor. My parents don't talk to me directly about what is happening in their marriage. It's almost as if they still look at me as the little girl who would crawl into their bed every night because I was afraid of the dark. That little girl used to find comfort and safety with her parents, but she wouldn't find those now.

One night, while I tried to doze off to sleep, my parents began another one of their fights. For some reason, instead of trying to block out the noise like usual, I decided to listen in just this once. I caught snippets of the argument, and from what I could put together, my dad was caught cheating with a younger woman from his work. An anonymous letter was sent to his company's human resources department describing the affair in great detail. I assume that's what led to him losing his job.

My mom has been brokenhearted and angry ever since —and rightfully so. I would be pissed too if my husband cheated on me. She's turned to wine to drown her sorrows, which is starting to become an issue. It's not like she drinks every night, so I'm not even sure if she needs help or where I would begin to find help for her. Sometimes she gets so drunk that she says hurtful things to me, and we end up fighting and not talking for days. During the last drunken argument my mom started with me, she told me she never even wanted kids. I was so hurt that I gave her the silent treatment for two weeks. Feeling so unwanted was one thing, but her validating my feelings? That was a samurai sword straight through the middle of my heart. What drove the blade in deeper was that she didn't even remember it the next day. She never apologized.

It's a shame because I love the person my mom is when she's not drunk.

Last night, she lightly tapped on my closed bedroom door. It was about midnight, and I was still up, mindlessly scrolling through MySpace as I listened to New Found Glory.

"Yup, I'm up," I responded to the tap.

My mom slowly entered the room. I looked up from my laptop to find her lingering in the doorway, still holding the knob as if she was hesitant to step inside. I quickly glanced between her and my screen, the laptop covering my face from where I sat behind my desk.

"I know, I know. I was just logging off and turning off the music. I couldn't sleep, and I was waiting for Taylor to call me." I knew she was coming in to say lights out. She didn't do it every night in the summer, but that was usually the only reason for her visits.

My mom fully entered the room and closed the door behind her. I watched her cautiously make her way to my bed. I kept my eyes low, pretending to stare intently at the screen in front of me. I studied my mom from under my dark eyelashes. She's a tiny woman, short and thin but curvy in the chest and bum. When I was little, I thought she was the prettiest lady I had ever seen, and I couldn't wait to grow up to look like her. Her big brown eyes are the mirror image of mine, but last night, and more recently—almost every night—they were bloodshot and puffy. Her thin lips were curved into a soft scold, like she was mad and sad. Her brown hair with caramel highlights was pulled back into a messy ponytail, and it looked like she hadn't washed it in days.

My mom gently took a seat on the corner of my bed, facing me. She didn't say anything for a minute, so I looked up to find her staring at me with a tight-lipped half grin on her face.

"Cora, I need to talk to you about what's going to happen with this house and your future," she said to me, in all seriousness.

I stopped scrolling the internet and looked up at her with concern. "Okay . . ."

"Your father is leaving. He has fallen in love with someone else. I've tried to make it work and change his mind, but I just can't and I'm sorry." Her voice cracked. Her shoulders began to jerk up and down as she tried to hold in her sob.

I ran to her on the bed and put my arms around her shoulders. She threw her hands to her face as if she could hide her tears and the pain that was radiating from her.

"I don't know what to say to you to make you feel better. This fucking kills me too, Mom. I hate him for ruining our lives, and I will stand by you no matter what. I know it may not seem like I know what's happening between you two, or that I have no interest, but I do. I hear it every night, and I see you and I see him. I don't agree with what Dad is doing, so I will take your side, always."

My mom looked at me through the tears in her eyes and simply said, "Don't." She gently patted my hand, then rose to head for the door. But before she left my room, she stopped and looked over her shoulder at me. "Cora, I'm sorry if I've failed you. Everything I've done, I've done for you. I love you." She walked out and gently closed the door behind her.

I sat still on the bed, staring at the door with her words echoing in my mind. I thought about her comment all night, but also about how my life would be changing from here on out.

Now, as I lie in the hammock, I'm still thinking about it. I didn't have time to ask her what she meant by "don't." I'm not sure what she was referring to . . . Does she not want me to stand by her? Does she not want me to hate my dad? I don't know, but I plan on asking her at some point.

I have been bored out of my mind for the past month because my best friend, Taylor, has been gone. Every summer, her family drives to Ohio to spend time with her grandparents. She hates it just as much as I do.

Taylor and I live for our summers together in Portland. When Taylor is home, we are usually at the beach or walking around downtown, browsing the bookstore. We typically end up reading our books on the patio of a café as we slowly sip on iced coffees.

Mmm, maybe I should get up and go get an iced coffee . . .

So I do just that. I roll out of the hammock and make my way to the back sliding doors. I enter the kitchen and grab my keys off the hook. Before I step out to go to my car, my mom comes down the stairs.

"Hey, Cora, where are you going?" she asks, standing on

the last stair. She's still in her pajamas, her hair still looks dirty, and the bags under her eyes are dark, almost black against her pale skin.

"Just running out to get an iced coffee. I'm bored and can't stand it any longer."

She shakes her head in an almost-comical way and walks past me toward the kitchen. "You and your iced coffees. While you're out, would you mind stopping and grabbing yourself some dinner for tonight? I'm busy so I won't be able to cook you something."

"Mmhmm, sure thing." I walk out and close the door behind me as I chuckle to myself. I have been cooking my own dinners for a while now. I guess she really isn't here at all, even when she is. I can't fault her for that since her whole life has drastically changed. My dad has been staying in a hotel for the past six months, but he comes home every so often to grab clothes or talk to my mom or spend time with me, briefly. It will be interesting to see how my mom handles going back to work in a week. As an administrator at the elementary school, she will be plenty busy with the new school year. Honestly, getting out of the house and keeping her mind occupied would be the best solution for her. I'm secretly wishing it also helps with her nighttime drinking habits. I can only hope.

I drive with all the windows down and turn my radio up as loud as my ears can stand it. "Alcohol and Altar Boys" by Bayside blasts through the speakers and the wind tosses my hair. I love my car and I love driving it. There's something soothing to me about being behind the wheel, alone with my thoughts and music.

Most people think I'm spoiled (and I am) because my dad bought me a used and fairly new 2003 Volkswagen Jetta when I turned sixteen. My parents praised me for my good grades and for being a great daughter, but I never expected them to buy me the car. But to my surprise, they got me the bright-blue five-speed manual transmission 1.8T Jetta I had shown them about eight thousand times leading up to my birthday. I take pride in my car, and I enjoy taking care of it. My dad taught me everything I need to know about vehicle maintenance. We bonded over washing it in the driveway, checking the oil and the tire pressure, making sure there was enough windshield washer fluid . . . all the things dads are supposed to teach you about taking care of your first car. I enjoyed our time in the driveway together, talking about cars and life. I wish I could have those days back.

I zoom downtown and back. Now satisfied to have an iced coffee, I spend the rest of the day trapped in my room, downloading music, making mix CDs, and browsing MySpace and useless stuff on the internet. After hours of mindless scrolling and with my eyes screaming at me, I break away from my room to head downstairs to cook myself dinner and watch TV.

When it hits midnight, I make my way upstairs and remember that Taylor comes home tomorrow. I start taking the stairs two at a time and run and jump onto my bed. Glancing at my phone, I see there are no new messages, so I place it on my bedside table. I click off the lamp next to my bed and the room goes dark. I relax my mind and end up drifting off to sleep thinking about sitting at the beach listening to the waves crash on the rocks. Picturing my mom and dad sitting in lounge chairs with smiles on their faces and drinks in their hands . . . like they used to when I was five.

CHAPTER TWO

The Restrictions

The next morning, I wake up feeling unrested with heavy eyes. I roll over and pat my bedside table to find my phone without looking. When I pick it up, I see Taylor has finally texted me: *Cora! I missed you so much! The Restrictions are playing tonight at Cal's at 9, you down? I can't wait to see you, so I need to see you TONIGHT!*

I respond: *Heck yes! I'll grab you at 8:30.*

I slowly pull the covers off myself to get out of bed. I make my way out of my room and down the stairs to the kitchen. As I'm fixing myself a bowl of cereal, I design an outfit for tonight in my head . . . even though I know I'll probably change five times before I settle on what to wear. I devour my breakfast and head back to my room. I spend the day rearranging my CDs, picking out an outfit, and updating my MySpace profile until six o'clock and then decide to take my time putting myself together for the show tonight.

I've just finished applying the last shade of eyeshadow on my lids when I stand back and take in the reflection of myself. My large oval-shaped brown eyes are perfectly outlined in black eyeliner with a light-purple eye shadow that stands out against my ivory skin. I'm wearing Taylor's favorite T-shirt of all time: a tight black sleeveless top with a thick camo hem that hugs my hips and accentuates my curves. My shoulder-length hair is dark brown with my signature bright-red streaks, and it is now perfectly styled and flipped out. It's my mission in life to try to emulate Rachael Leigh Cook's hair in *Josie and the Pussycats*, and I think I've started to master it.

I've always been uncomfortable about my body. I was one of the first girls in school to get boobs and their period in one go at the age of ten. I spent most of my middle school years wearing baggy sweatshirts and jeans that were a size or two too big for me. I was always more comfortable in shorts and a T-shirt while swimming because I hated the way my arms looked a bit "too big" and how my thighs touched. Now that I'm getting older, I'm realizing that my body is nothing to be ashamed of. Once when I was fourteen, I was trying to cover myself up at the beach, and I remember standing with my toes just hitting the water, afraid to get my clothes wet. My grandma came and stood next to me. She tickled my hip and said, "Honey, you won't be young forever. Don't hide yourself. You're beautiful. Don't be so shy, life's too short." Since that day, I've slowly been building up my confidence, and I've come a long way. Sometimes I even allow myself some cleavage . . . but I still won't wear a bikini. Maybe someday.

I fix the cuffs of my light-blue jeans so they rest perfectly over my black-and-white checkered Vans. One last look in the mirror and I decide I'm good to go.

I pull in front of Taylor's house at 8:20 p.m. I finished getting ready earlier than I had expected and was growing impatient sitting around the house. Not finding anything to do while I waited, I ate a couple of slices of cold pizza left over in the fridge. When I was done, I headed out. Taylor won't mind that I got here a bit early.

I park my car next to the curb, turn my music down, and beep the horn twice. Taylor swings open her front door and is fidgeting with her purse. It hangs open on her shoulder while she holds a sandwich in the other hand. She waves her pinky finger of the hand that's gripping the sandwich at me with a huge shit-eating grin on her face. Taylor Walsh is up to no good . . . but then again, she's never up to any good. After she closes the front door, I watch her saunter down her driveway, focused on eating the sandwich, trying not to get any on her face with each bite. I take note of what Taylor is wearing to verify that I'm neither overdressed nor underdressed. She's sporting her signature light-blue flared jeans with huge slashes that expose both her knees, leaving some fringe hanging on the sides. A black tank top paired with a white T-shirt underneath fits snugly to her torso. Her neck is adorned with her favorite black beaded necklace, which hangs down just above her belly button. The outfit is completed with a pair of black flip-flops that I rarely see her *not* wearing . . . even in the winter, with snow.

I relax and feel comfortable in my outfit once I see Taylor's. It almost looks as though we coordinated our clothing, but I guess that's what happens when you've been best friends with someone for years. You start to take on some of their characteristics and style—but I will never acquire Taylor's height, which is a total bummer. I will be short forever. Taylor is a tall girl, exceedingly taller than me;

in fact, she looks like she could be my older sister when we stand side by side. She has natural strawberry-blond hair, almond-shaped gray eyes, and considering she's a ginger, not many freckles on her fair skin. I will never forget when, a couple of years ago, her dad took us to Key West on vacation. Taylor and I were lounging by the pool when Mr. Walsh, accompanied by his fiancée at the time, approached us. His fiancée gave Taylor an earful about how she didn't have sunscreen on and that it was immature of her. It ended up being a heated (and awkward) fight. You know the one: "You're not my mom," blah, blah, blah. Taylor regretted it later when her skin was as red as a crab. She spent the rest of the night lying in our hotel bed in pain and could barely move. Since that day, she's been adamant about covering herself with sunscreen anytime she's out in the summer sun.

I met Taylor when we were in seventh grade. We were both waiting outside the school for the first bell to ring. For some reason, our middle school made students wait outside in the morning until the first bell . . . I never understood why, and I still don't. Anyway, I was standing next to my neighbor at the time, Katelyn, when it started raining. Katelyn spotted an umbrella in the crowd and told me to follow her to whoever was holding it. When we made it to the umbrella, twelve-year-old Taylor was standing underneath, shivering. I remember seeing her and thinking she was so cool and pretty because her makeup was perfect and her mom didn't make her wear a jacket. I wasn't allowed to wear makeup until I was fourteen, so Taylor was fascinating to me. Taylor leaned the umbrella over and asked us if we wanted to get under. Since that day, we've been best friends—inseparable.

Taylor shoves the rest of the sandwich in her mouth and swings my car door open. "Lady! I'm so happy to see you. I've missed you so *freaking* much, and I have news," she squeals out excitedly between chews.

"Whoa, okay. I've missed you. Don't leave me again. And spill the fucking news," I say.

"Okay, so remember when Lars from The Restrictions sent me a MySpace message asking me to hang with him sometime? Well, girl, I messaged him, told him we will be seeing him tonight, and he wants me to hang around after they perform so we can talk!" Taylor is facing me in the passenger seat clapping her hands together and laughing like a little schoolgirl.

She's been crushing on Lars since we saw his band perform about two months ago. Lars is the drummer for The Restrictions, and he just graduated this year from Essex High. In the brief moment we spoke with him, he mentioned that The Restrictions have some local gigs this summer but have signed on to tour with a popular ska band next summer. Taylor has been smitten with him ever since. I'm not as excited as her because this means I'll have to awkwardly hang in the background while they flirt until she's ready to call it a night. I'm shy, so I don't meet many people when we go out. I'm also socially awkward and I have a hard time opening up to new people. So this usually leaves me acting as the third wheel to Taylor and her date.

"That's sweet! I'll be your wingwoman," I respond with a fake, gleeful smile. Taylor doesn't notice the fakeness and I'm glad. I want her to be happy.

We pull up to Cal's at nine o'clock on the dot. It's a small dive bar where a lot of local pop/punk bands perform—and one of the very few bars that allow anyone under eighteen to attend. The parking lot is full and littered with people hanging around cars, smoking cigarettes, and just shooting the shit. Everyone is dressed like they are a member in the band. I pull into a space and throw the car in park.

"Let's do this!" Taylor says as she wiggles her eyebrows with that damn mischievous smile again.

Fuck. I'm in for a long night.

We walk in and pay. The bouncer at the door gives Taylor and me the infamous brand on our hands of a large *X* in permanent marker. The *X*s scream, "We are underage! Don't look at us, serve us, or breathe near us." As the ink dries on my hand, I take in the familiar scene. For the past two years that I've been coming to Cal's, nothing has changed. According to my parents and other locals, it's been like this since the eighties. There are old tin beer advertisements on the walls, along with some framed photos of "regulars" posing next to Cal. The stools at the bar are red vinyl with slabs of duct tape across tears in the fabric. The air always smells like stale beer, lingering cigarette smoke, and, my personal favorite, sweat. It's so strong, but for some reason, you get used to it. Same with the stickiness of the floors and how your shoes get stuck if you don't move around periodically. It sounds super shitty, but I always have a good time at Cal's.

Taylor grabs my hand and weaves me through the small crowd of people until we are in front of the stage but off to the left in our own little corner. The room darkens and the band walks on to take their positions. Light floods the stage again when the band members are settled and have their instruments in hand. Except the singer doesn't hold an instrument; he holds a microphone, which I guess you could consider his instrument.

"Hello, Portland! We are The Restrictions, and we are here to play some shit for you!" the singer screams into the microphone. Immediately after, the band starts up and straight into the first song. Taylor is watching Lars with wide eyes and a smirk on her face. I can tell by that look, she's already in love, but that's not unusual for her. Taylor and I are opposites, and that's why we work. She's outspoken, I'm shy. She's tall, I'm short. She's a flirt, I don't know how to flirt. She applies herself without trying, I have to work at it. She falls in love at first sight, but it takes me some time. We just make sense and I think that's why we are best friends. I wish I could be more like Taylor, though. I've tried to be carefree and talk to boys without worrying what they think . . . but I just can't. I get too nervous, and I end up crumpling into a huge ball of anxiety and crawling back home.

Instead, I people watch in crowds. I like to scan the masses and observe how everyone reacts to the music, the band, the atmosphere. After watching the band play for a while, I keep feeling like someone is staring at me, so I survey the crowd again to see if it's just in my head. I figure it's someone who caught me looking at them first, so they are returning the favor, but I don't see anyone looking this way. I decide to turn my attention back to the stage and that's when it hits me. On stage right, in front of Taylor and me, is the bassist. He's staring directly at me while his fingers work his bass guitar like it's nothing, like he doesn't even have to think about it.

He's tall, taller than the rest of the members in the band. He has slicked-back jet-black hair with a streak of bright pink down the right side.

His eyes though. How did I miss this boy with those eyes?

Bright topaz-blue eyes that are soft but also mysterious and mischievous stare right into me. He's wearing a black band T-shirt with fitted dark jeans. Tattoos cover his golden skin on the backs of both hands and all the way up his left arm into the sleeve of his T-shirt. As I study him, up and down, I lock eyes with him again. I immediately avert my gaze to the singer as a grin stretches across my face. My cheeks are hot, and I know they're blood red. I feel like I'm going to explode like a tomato in a microwave with all this blood pumping to my face. My heart is pounding so fast and hard that I can hear it in my ears, to the point where it feels like the drummer is playing my heartbeat aloud for the crowd to hear.

Get it together, Cora. Guys don't look at you—you probably have something on your face or your hair looks stupid.

I nervously pat my cheeks and wipe my lips, but I don't feel anything there. I wait a second and then smooth the top of my hair down with my hands.

Okay, perfect. You're fixed.

I slowly turn to look at him again, and luckily he's not looking at me anymore. This time, he's focused on his hands plucking at the strings on the bass guitar. I'm admiring him play and taking in the tattoos on his hands and his arm, when suddenly Taylor bumps my shoulder and jerks me from my thoughts. I turn to see her smirking with one brow arched high on her forehead. My face goes rigid as I mouth

"WHAT?" with my arms open, palms faceup.

She leans and shouts into my ear, "Bass boy's got it bad," and then kisses my cheek before going back to her own admiring of Lars.

My palms become sweaty. I'm nervous—too nervous to function. She noticed him watching me, so I'm not making this up. Is this what it's like when a guy checks you out? I'm about to have an anxiety attack, so I make my way to the bathroom. I bust through the women's room door and stand in front of a sink. Taylor enters not a second later behind me.

"Oh my god. Cora has a suitor," Taylor teases and then clicks her tongue.

"A suitor? What are you, a host for a dating show?" I'm projecting, hoping she won't notice that this guy and those eyes got me. I'm hooked.

"What do you want me to call him? A lover? Look, this is perfect for us. I can chat with Lars, and you can chat with Pinky."

"Pinky?" I ask her in a flat tone.

"Yeah, the hair. Duh!" she rolls her eyes at me.

"Okay, I don't know what I'm doing. I'm not good at this and I'm going to drown in a bucket of my own sweat." I'm starting to babble as I check my armpits in the mirror to make sure the black of my shirt is hiding any sweat spots. So far, so good.

"Run cold water on your wrists. Then stand up tall and look in the mirror. You are fucking gorgeous. Guys at our school are stupid. And I mean, c'mon, Cora, let's be real, you don't talk much," Taylor levels with me. "But you've got this, you've been with guys before. Plus, I will be with you the whole time. So please, if he approaches you, just talk to him."

I'm running the cold water on my wrists while flicking my eyes between Taylor and my reflection. I finally shut off the water, snatch some paper towels, and study myself in the mirror as I dry my hands.

You can do this. Taylor is here.

"You're right. He may not even find me and talk to me. I'm not going to worry . . . yet," I respond as I toss the paper towels in the trash. I miss, so I bend over and pick them up to *place* them in the trash.

Taylor puts her hands on my shoulders from behind me when I stand back up. She moves me back out of the bathroom door and into the crowd. We make our way back to our spot at the side of the stage. As soon as we get back, the band stops playing.

"That was our last song. Again, we are The Restrictions. Thank you and goodnight!" the singer shouts as he swipes his sweaty light-brown hair across his face in an attempt to move it off his eyes.

Taylor whips out her Motorola Razr phone and immediately shoots off a text. She continues to hold her phone, staring at the screen like she's waiting for a response. She begins clicking at the buttons again before smacking her flip phone shut and shoving it in her back pocket. "Lars said he's going to meet us at the bar once he's cleaned up and put his equipment away. Let's hang at the bar and grab some sodas."

I don't even know if I responded, but we are moving. Taylor has my hand again as we weave through the crowd to the bar. She orders us two Cokes and we stand off to the side.

As we are sipping our drinks and discussing the logistics of driving schedules for senior year, the crowd parts and Lars walks toward us, taking his place next to Taylor.

Lars is an attractive guy, to put it simply. He's the same height as Taylor but he's thin—you know, the type who probably eats a ton but doesn't gain a pound . . . like ever. He has shoulder-length bleach-blond hair, dark-brown eyes, and a silver ring that stands out on his perfectly golden-tan nose. He gives off more of a surfer vibe than punk rocker, but it works for him and the band.

Taylor introduces us, forgetting we've already met. After we engage in small talk and I tell him how good the band sounded, Taylor cuts right to the chase with the flirting, leaving me to stand off on my own with my soda in hand. I take two large final sips as I pretend to kick something on the ground, periodically looking around at the photos and vintage ads on the walls (as if I haven't seen them a million times already), before I turn to place the empty glass back on the bar. As I spin back around, I hit a wall. A tall, hard, semi-wet, fantastic-smelling wall.

"Oh, dear god. I'm sorry, so sorry," I say as I step back and look up to find those topaz eyes from earlier, staring down at me with a hint of amusement in them. One brow quickly cocks up and down in a flirtatious manner. My eyes trail down his face to a soft grin that makes me weak in the knees.

"No, really, I should be sorry. I leaned in to get your attention and forgot that humans move," Pinky responds with a soft laugh as a black strand of hair falls to his forehead. He shoves his hand through his hair, trying to put the piece back into place. I finally realize I'm just standing in front of him, wide-eyed and staring. I haven't said anything for a solid fifteen seconds.

"C-c-cora. Cora Mitchell. Friends and family call me Cece... sometimes. It was my grandma's name and my mom wanted to keep the name alive. She says it's unique, like me," I finish, accentuating the *q* in *unique*. Not even sure why I told him that last bit.

"Jeremiah Novak. People call me Miah. I don't think I've seen you at any of our shows before," Miah responds to my stuttering foolishness.

"I'm shy. I mean, what? Yes, I'm shy so I tend to blend in with the crowds, but tonight my friend Taylor wanted us practically on the stage with you."

Good Lord, I'm so stupid.

Miah chuckles, which puts my nerves at ease, kind of. "I really like your shoes. I'm a Vans guy," he says as he lifts a leg and shows me his Vans slip-ons. His are black with traditional tattoo–style red roses on them.

"Oh my god, I love those! Very nice, and I'm very jealous."

He nods his head at my response, with a large half smile on his face. "Did you want another drink? I was just going to grab a Red Bull."

"Umm, I'm all set. Thank you, though."

Miah leans on the bar and orders a Red Bull. He turns to face me again with his drink in his hand. I nervously look down at my feet, not sure of what to talk about next.

Quick, think of something to say. Don't be an idiot. Don't be weird, oh god, don't be weird!

"What school do you go to?" I blurt out.

He blows out a small laugh before answering, "Um, the

school of work, I guess?"

I'm confused by his response, so I chew on it in my mind for a second.

"I didn't mean that in a rude way. It's just, I'm twenty-two so I haven't attended high school for a while." There it is, I knew this was too good to be true. I'm talking to a twenty-two-year-old man. Perfect. I mean, what did I expect? Things never work out for me in the guy department. I'm going to be alone forever.

As I'm spiraling in my mind, he notices my deflation and my awkward silence.

"Um, I hope that doesn't disappoint you. How old are you?" he responds with hesitation. I can tell he's nervous now. He's started to grip his Red Bull can tighter, making the aluminum pop in his hand.

"I'm seventeen," I reply with uncertainty, and my hands start to sweat again.

He steps closer to me as a tight-lipped smile appears on his face.

"Well, Cora, it's always nice to meet a new friend. Would it be cool if I got your number, to text and keep in touch?"

I don't even give it a second. Something in my gut is telling me to say yes. Maybe it's not even my gut, but my heart. Whatever it is, I'm barely thinking, and I wouldn't even listen to it if it were screaming "NO!" and waving huge red flags. Something about Jeremiah is just different.

"I would totally be okay with that." I can't contain my smile.

We both pull out our cell phones from our pockets to exchange numbers when Taylor and Lars approach us.

Taylor extends her hand out to Miah as she declares, "I'm Taylor, Cece's BFF. Don't hurt her or I'll hurt you."

Miah laughs, totally unphased by Taylor's death threat. "Miah. I really hope mine and Cece's friendship never leads to hurt."

Taylor turns to me with her brows high on her head. After a beat, she says to me, "Curfew. We gotta go." Her head swivels back to Miah and Lars, "It was very nice to meet you, Miah. Lars, call me tomorrow?"

I awkwardly wave and smirk at Miah. He returns the wave along with a wink that sends my heart into my stomach.

I really hope he texts me . . .

CHAPTER THREE

This Is It

September 2005

Today is the first day of my last year in high school. I couldn't be happier. Traditionally, my parents would hang around, have breakfast with me, and send me off wishing me a great start to the year. This year, my mom is out the door and heading to work at the elementary school bright and early. I assume she's avoiding any possibility of crossing paths with my dad, but he found a new job last week and starts today, so I don't expect him to stop by.

Taylor and I decided last week that we would carpool Mondays and Fridays, the two days she doesn't have field hockey after school. Oh yeah, Taylor's an athlete. Another opposite of ours. I love running, so that's how I stay active, but school teams were never my thing. Being competitive is not my forte.

In the kitchen, I pack my cross-body satchel (the same one I've used for the past three years) with a notebook and some pens, and I toss in a few mechanical pencils for good measure. I also pack a granola bar, a water bottle, and a snack-size bag of pretzels. If I get hungry, I'll just grab something from the cafeteria. I stocked up my car last night too, with an extra change of clothes, a pair of shoes, and some tampons. You can never be too prepared.

I finish up my bowl of cereal and down a small glass of SunnyD, grab my bag, and head out the door. I step outside and get chills down my back. The air is cool and I can see my breath. I should have grabbed a sweatshirt, but I know by noon I'll be sweating, so there's no point. I turn on the heat for the morning ride and mentally remind myself to turn on the air conditioning before I get out because it will be hot once I get back into my car in the afternoon.

I turn down Taylor's street and see that she's waiting outside on the curb for me. Large sunglasses cover her eyes, and slung over her shoulder is a large purse that carries her books and whatever else. She's got her mischievous smile in place as soon as she sees my car approaching.

"Hey girl, heyyyy," she sings, sliding into the passenger seat. She looks at me and pulls her sunglasses to the bridge of her nose. "You look dead-ass tired. Everything okay?"

"Yeah, just up late," I answer, smiling largely.

"So things are heating up with Miah? I knew it! You'll never be able to stay 'just friends,'" she says as she puts air quotes around *just friends*.

"Look, there's a huge age gap here and he's being respectful. I do really like him, but I won't pursue anything until we both confess that we want something more and that our age difference won't come between us. Plus, my parents will croak if I bring him home and then croak again once I tell them his age."

"I get it. I'm just very interested in seeing where this goes,"

Taylor says, winking at me.

It doesn't take us long to get to Rock Point High from Taylor's house, about a ten-minute drive. Once I pull into the school's designated senior lot, I park the car. Before Taylor and I get out, we look at each other. With a heavy sigh, I say, "This is it. Our last year..."

"Let's make it a year to remember," she finishes as she snorts and then rolls her eyes. That's what our other classmates have been declaring to us when we've bumped into them around town this summer... It's so cliché. I laugh and we both jump out of the car and walk into school for the first day of our last year as high school students.

* * *

Taylor and I both make it through the final bell... barely. Waking up early after summer vacation is the worst, but we have lunch together and took the opportunity to go out and grab some coffees for a jolt of caffeine. We also share the same free block after lunch and our last block of the day, so it makes school infinitely more bearable.

Overall, day one of senior year went off without a hitch. There were no embarrassing moments for me, but the usual rumor mill is working overtime with all the gossip from the summer. I'm never part of it because I don't go to parties or socialize with anyone else in the school other than Taylor. On occasion, we hang with a few other people in school whom we've met through local gigs, but they aren't the gossiping type.

I'm finally home when my phone goes off. I immediately

open it and see that Miah has texted me: *Hey, I remembered that you get out at 2 and I wanted to see how your first day went. I've been dying to text you all day.*

My heart is pounding hard, and my hands start sweating. Miah and I have been texting for over a week, but I still get so nervous responding to him. Like I'm going to make a total fool of myself. I move my fingers over the keypad, but I don't press any buttons. I'm just thinking of what to say. Finally, I send off a reply: *It was a good day, but I still hate school.*

Aww, c'mon. It's not so bad. I bet you have a line of boys who are eager to see you every day.

My face gets hot and red all the way to the tips of my ears reading his text, and then my heart sinks. The only boy I would like to see every day is Miah, but I can't tell him that. Plus, the fact that he thinks guys are into me is endearing. I've had two boyfriends in my life, but I don't think you can count the kid you date when you're eleven . . . he was more like my best friend. I'm not a prude, though—I enjoy kissing, but I haven't found anyone who makes me feel like I'm ready to lose myself entirely for him. I don't want things to get messy, so I avoid confrontation at all costs.

I text Miah back: *Ugh, not really. I'm not "popular" enough. Plus, I wouldn't even care if there were a line of boys wanting me.*

Hmm, Little Jetta. Are you telling me you've already snatched a boy for yourself who was in that line?

Miah's favorite new nickname for me is "Little Jetta." He thinks it's funny how much pride I take in my car and keeping it in pristine condition. God, I would hate for him to see my bedroom, especially my alphabetized CD collection.

Nah. I had one boyfriend freshman year. We made it 11

months when I realized that I don't want to date while in high school. Too much drama, and high school boys are SO immature.

Well, good thing I'm not in high school. Right, Little Jetta?

As soon as I read his text, my mouth flops open and I reread his words over and over again. Does this mean he wants to, like . . . go on a date?

I'm just about to send a text back when I hear the front door close behind me. I jump and my phone flies out of my hands across the hallway floor. I turn and see my dad standing awkwardly with empty flattened boxes under his arm.

"Hey, I didn't think you would be home so soon after your first day. Uh, how did it go?" he says to me as I'm bending to snatch up my phone. My dad's name is Peter Mitchell. He's a tall man with short dark hair, which he always has neatly styled so that only a few white strands stand out. He has brown eyes like my mom and me, but his are a darker chocolate shade. His skin is always tan, even in the winter—he just enjoys being outside and always being busy. When I was younger, I used to love watching him fix things, or work in the vegetable garden, or hang Christmas lights. He's so smart, and he seems to know everything. But right now, he's visibly nervous as his hand is continuously clinking his keys in his pants pocket. I'm nervous too but it doesn't offset the lingering tension between us.

"Uh, no, I had no reason to stick around, so I'm home. I'm just about to do some homework."

He wipes his feet and enters the house to approach me. "Look, I didn't want to do this while you were here, but your mom has officially kicked me out and asked me to come grab all my things. This won't take long, but I'd prefer it if you didn't watch me," he says, and then lets out a large sigh.

"Yeah, yeah, okay." Well, that brought me down from my Miah-high really quickly. My heart clenches and I begin to feel cold. Miah just had that same heart in my chest feeling so alive for the first time in a long time, and another man—the one who is supposed to protect my heart—just managed to make me feel like I was dying inside.

I make the climb up the stairs to my room and shut the door behind me. I lie on the bed and my eyes begin to burn as I let out a sob. A million thoughts run through my mind: *How did it get this way? Why does this happen to good women? Will this be my future? Since all marriages are like this, I'm never going to get married. And just for extra measure, I'll never have kids.*

When I wake up, I realize I ended up sobbing myself to sleep for an hour. I roll off the mattress and head to my bedroom door. I try to hear if my dad's still lingering about the house and packing up his shit, but I don't hear anything, so I open the door. I'm passing the bay window in the hall when I see movement in the driveway. I stand and watch as my dad loads his boxes into the back of his SUV.

That officially stops my heart.

I hated my parents always fighting, but I guess when you're young, you think your parents are together forever and they will never split up, regardless of what comes their way. Disney princesses put these images in my mind of true love lasting forever, but you never actually see the princesses living their best lives with Prince Charming when they are old and wrinkly. Seeing and hearing my parents fight and finding out that my dad cheated on my mom have left my heart and mind very confused about how love should be.

They've been fighting out in the open for a solid two years. I've had all that time to come to the realization that I don't want to get married, and I never want to have kids because I don't want them to go through this pain that I feel. It's scary but it makes me angry too. I hate my dad for what he's done to my mom, but I hate my mom for exploding the way she does and giving him a reaction when he doesn't deserve one. Standing here watching him pack his life into his car without the slightest bit of remorse on his face made me realize I've hidden the key to my heart somewhere I forgot. Maybe someday I'll find it again.

Later that night, my mom comes home. She's been hanging out with "the girls" a lot since she found out my dad's been cheating. When she goes out, her nights consist of meeting her friends at a bar, having wine for dinner, getting dropped off, and then having wine for a late-night snack in the sunroom. She sits in the sunroom until she eventually makes her way to bed. What she does back there—well, besides drink wine—I have no idea.

I enter the kitchen and find her pouring a glass of wine.

"Did you see your father today?" she asks coldly without even turning toward me.

"Yeah, he packed some stuff and was out of here pretty quickly." I wait for a few moments, but she doesn't respond.

Slowly moving to face me with her glass that's brimming with wine, she speaks again, "How was school?"

"Uh, it was okay. How was work?"

"It was okay. Music and laptop off at ten tonight. No later. I hope your dad removed all his stuff that he needed from the house because I will be having the locks changed. I have to call your aunt Karen before I head to bed, so I'll be up later. Goodnight, Cece," she says with a hard frown she wears a lot these days. She turns and heads toward the sunroom.

I slowly make the trek up to my room. As my foot hits the top stair, my phone vibrates in my sweatpants pocket: *Hey, did I say something wrong? I don't want to come off as clingy or annoying in any way, but you kinda just stopped texting. I also wanted to make sure you were okay.*

I read Miah's text and smile. But my smile fades as I contemplate what to send back to him. *Do I tell him the truth and air my dirty laundry so soon? Do I lie?*

I think about it for a few minutes before replying: *Nothing you said, honestly. Without getting into it, I was thrown into a situation with my parents today and I couldn't get back to you. Thank you for checking in on me. How was your day?*

He sends back: *It was chill as usual. Worked until 4, band practice, and then hung with the guys back at the house.*

Before I can follow up, another message comes through: *Question, would you want to come hang at our house Saturday, October 1st? We're having a party and the band is going to play. I don't drink and neither do the other guys, but there will be alcohol . . . if you're into that.*

How the heck am I going to run this by my mom? I sit on my bed, looking at my phone, trying to come up with a solution. I know just the person who can help me handle this.

Taylor, I need a favor . . . Miah just invited me to a party at his house. How do I get Lucy to agree or maybe not know what we're really doing? And you are coming with me, that's not a question.

Taylor likes to call my mom by her first name. Taylor always says that she was a Lucy in another life.

I wait for two minutes before Taylor responds: *YES, BITCH. Tell Lucy we are going to a show and we will be back later. She won't think twice about it. You are way too nervous if you didn't think of that. Calm your shit down!*

On it. Thanks! Love you.

I flip back to Miah's text and type my answer: *Yeah, I would love that! Is it cool to bring Taylor along?*

Sick. Yeah, bring her. Party starts at 8. Text you later. Night, Cora, sweet dreams.

Ugh, I've never had a boy say sweet dreams, and just like everything else with Miah, I never want anyone else to say it to me unless it's him.

CHAPTER FOUR

A Party with a Painting

October 2005

Taylor and I arrive at Lars and Miah's party around 8:30 p.m. All four band members in The Restrictions live together in an old Victorian house about three blocks from downtown Portland. Once we enter, Taylor and I are both surprised to find that the house is in pristine condition and spotless. Almost cleaner than my house, and my mom scrubs the floors on her hands and knees. Standing in the kitchen, I can see the house is overflowing with people and they're funneling into the backyard. The lawn has tiki torches along the sides of a fence lining the property. There's a small stage with band equipment set up in the back of the yard and a floodlight shining on it.

Taylor and I ease our way through the crowd gathered in the kitchen to find ourselves some drinks. I'm not into alcohol, so I stick to my usual: a Coke. Taylor treats herself to Coke with a splash of rum since I drove. Her mom is away for work, and we are crashing at her place tonight. Apparently, my mom checking out on parenting duties in favor of wine and "the girls" has its perks.

Just as we turn to awkwardly stand and people watch (we know absolutely no one here), I see Miah's black-and-pink hair enter the kitchen through the crowd. He's pretty much the tallest person at the party, so he's hard to miss. People are saying hello, and he returns each greeting. Every partygoer he approaches seems excited to see him, and I smile as I bite the brim of my red Solo cup. Noticing the way people admire him makes my cheeks flush and my heart pump faster. It's clear he is a good person—I see it, and other people seem to think so too.

Taylor bumps my arm with her elbow, but I don't react to her because I already know she's spotted him too. Miah turns as he's mid-conversation with a couple who are standing by the fridge across the kitchen, and he locks eyes with me. His piercing blue gaze cuts deep into me as a large smile paints his face, stretching from ear to ear. My right arm is slung around my stomach, tightly pulling at my shirt like I'm holding myself together, so I don't fall apart by how much my body reacts to him. My other hand is gripping my plastic cup still as I smile back and raise my drink like I'm giving a toast. I'm sweating—I can feel it dripping down my back.

Why did I just do that? Why not just let go of your shirt and wave like a normal person? Get it together, Cora. Breathe!

Miah returns his attention to the couple who haven't stopped talking to him since they cornered him. They all nod at each other and he starts to make his way toward us . . . toward me. Before I know it, he's standing in front of me with his hands awkwardly at his sides.

"Hey, you made it!" he says as he leans in for a hug. I jump and my drink sloshes a bit but doesn't spill.

Thank fuck.

I embrace him and damn, he smells good. Like a mixture of sandalwood, Red Bull, and fresh laundry. I've never appreciated the smell of clean clothes more than I do now. He also feels good—this feels right, like I really needed this hug and I didn't even know it. I'm not one for enjoying hugs, or people touching me in general, so when I resume my place next to Taylor and look over at her, her mouth is hanging open in shock. I roll my eyes.

"Am I missing something? An inside joke between you two? Why does Taylor look like she's seen a ghost?" Miah asks, his eyes shifting back and forth between the both of us.

"Oh me? I'm sorry, our little Cece here is not one for hugs, but seeing that exchange makes me think she's a liar. Now I'm going to be hugging her all the time," Taylor says.

"Well, well, Little Jetta's full of secrets. Isn't she?" Miah winks at me.

"You guys have nicknames and you never mentioned that to me either? What the hell, Cece!" Taylor shouts as she gently punches my arm. That gets people eying us, and I'm ready to melt into myself from embarrassment. Miah looks around, smiling at everyone, and then turns back to us. Just then, Lars appears next to Miah, who nods to his friend in a silent "What's up?"

"Taylor! Cora! You guys came, siiiiick!" Lars says as he grabs Taylor's hand. "I'm taking her away for a bit, if that's okay. I want to introduce her to some peeps."

I nod and smile at the both of them, acknowledging that it's okay. Once Lars and Taylor leave, Miah moves to the kitchen counter. "What are we drinking, Cora? Can I get you another?" he offers, shuffling around bottles to find the stack of cups.

"I'll do a refill on my Coke, please. The question is, what are you drinking, Miah? Should I be worried?" I hand him my empty cup, raising my eyebrows at him.

"Oh, I'm going hard in the paint tonight. I'm going to be doing shots all night!" he answers, pouring the soda into my cup. I begin to panic a bit as I think about how out of my element I am. Parties and drinking are so not my thing. This may be a sign that whatever hopes I had for Miah and me are going to be washed away, tonight.

When he notices I haven't responded, he turns and hands me my drink, "Calm down, Jetta, I'm joking. I told you I don't drink, remember?"

"Oh shit, that's right. Why don't you? Doesn't that add to the fun of being in a punk band? Getting wasted and ruining hotel rooms after shows and stuff?" I say, smiling to show him I'm kidding, although I am very curious as to why a twenty-two-year-old guy in a band doesn't drink alcohol.

"I started experimenting with drugs and alcohol when I was about your age, and that lasted until I was about twenty. I realized I didn't like the way any of it made me feel and it just wasn't for me. I'm not against it, and if it's something other people want to do, I would never stop anyone from living their lives. It's just not for me. So I drink a Red Bull or two to take the edge off or I smoke a cigarette."

My eyes grow wide with his confession. "Wow, I would have never guessed that you smoke. Oh and it's totally cool, by the way. I don't like drinking because I think it tastes terrible. So that's that."

"That's that," Miah agrees with a smirk as he shrugs his shoulders. Suddenly, he takes my hand. "Come here, I want to show you something."

I follow his lead as he pulls me through the crowded kitchen and stops in front of a closed door. "You may think this is dorky, but sometimes I have a lot of things going on in my mind, and I feel like I need to release those things. So, well . . . let me just show you." He opens the door but continues to hold my hand as we descend a dimly lit stairwell.

"You don't release the things in your head by murdering people, like *Texas Chainsaw Massacre*–style, right?" I ask nervously.

Miah bursts out a quick, mocking laugh. "No, but that movie is pretty sick."

"I agree. I love it," I say as I nod, like he can somehow see me from the back of his head.

We reach the bottom of the stairs, and Miah flicks a set of light switches. He drops my hand and moves farther into the basement as my eyes follow him. When he stops walking, he is standing in front of a large canvas sitting on an easel. I stare at the canvas with my mouth open, and it stares back at me. Painted on the canvas are two large, beautiful caramel-colored eyes with flecks of green speckled throughout the brown. They look like two fascinating marbles you would obsess over as a toddler.

"Miah! This is . . . this is amazing. Why would I ever think this is dorky? It is so beautiful." I walk closer to the canvas so that he and I are now side by side. His hand grazes mine and it feels electric. It sends chills up my arm, making the hair on the back of my neck stand up. He looks over at me and is staring at my profile, taking in my expression with a nervous smirk.

I wonder if he felt that too . . .

"Do you recognize them?" he probes apprehensively, voice shaking. I look at him confused. My brows stitch together trying to understand what he means. I study his eyes and then the ones on the canvas. I *have* seen those eyes, many times before—actually, for seventeen years I've seen those eyes.

"These are my eyes. But why? What would make you want to paint them?" I question, laughing in disbelief.

"I don't know how to say this because I don't want you to feel uncomfortable, but when I saw your eyes that night at Cal's, I felt like I had seen them before. We hadn't met yet—I know we hadn't—but your eyes tell your story, Cora. You have this calming yet playful energy about you that shows through your eyes. I was nervous to show you because I didn't want you to think I was crazy for painting a part of you after only meeting once, but I couldn't get them out of my mind."

I'm still staring at the painting, collecting my thoughts but also thinking about how to respond. I know I need to really think about what I want from Miah, but I've decided tonight's not the night for me to make that choice. Tonight, I want to get to know him, listen to his band play, and just enjoy the moment.

"The only thought that comes to my mind is how amazing this is. Actually, one more thought: What can't you do?" I say, turning to him.

"Well, umm, hmmm . . ." He gives it genuine thought and then answers, "I can't dance." He smiles and his shoulders drop from his ears, showing me that he has relaxed.

"You don't look like much of a dancer, so I believe it." I nod my head at him and we both laugh.

When we return to the party, we notice that everyone has filed outside. Miah looks at the time and realizes the band is about to perform. We walk into the night air and I find Taylor standing around a bunch of people talking loudly and laughing. I cross the yard to join her and hope she's not blasted drunk already.

"Coraaaaa!" Taylor says as she hugs me. "This is her. My best friend, my sister, and Miah's muse," she gushes to the group with a wink. I'm so embarrassed that I elbow her in the stomach to shut her up. She's definitely buzzed. She's well on her way to drunk.

One of the girls steps closer to me. "Ahh, so this is Cece. The girl with the big brown eyes. My name is Evie." She extends her hand out. I take it and she gives mine a firm shake, like we made a good business deal.

"Yup, that's me . . . I guess." I tuck my hair behind my ears shyly.

"I'm Miah's sister. Well, one of them, the youngest one, to be exact," she says with an eye roll.

Evie's tall, about Taylor's height. She has blond hair with a streak of pink like Miah's, and her tresses are coiffed in a tight pinup-girl updo. Her makeup style matches her hair, with winged eyeliner, pink cheeks, and bright-red lipstick that's striking against her alabaster skin. Evie is curvy, and her white fifties-style dress hugs her body flawlessly. The dress has a cherry design on it that matches her red lips. I can tell she's a badass chick, and someone I could see myself becoming friends with.

"I just want to say, I know there's this weird age gap between you both, but my family isn't like that. We aren't judgmental dicks. I don't know where this is going," she says, swirling her finger in a circle, "but my advice to you both: just let it be whatever it wants to be."

"Erm, well, thank you. But we've only hung out, like, twice, and we're still getting to know each other. I appreciate your approval, and we will see what happens," I respond without missing a beat.

I've been thinking about it a lot lately. With every text we send, every flirtatious remark, that stutter my heart makes when the image of Miah playing bass while staring at me comes into my mind. I can't get him out of my head, but that worry in the pit of my stomach forms, and it hardens like a fist. The uncertainty of my parents approving, what my classmates will think, him going to bars and clubs that I can't get into, him being able to go anywhere he wants without needing permission. I've thought about all of it, but I can't get ahead of myself just yet. Evie's right, I'm just going to let this be whatever it wants to be and try to push away that evil witch in my mind called doubt. Suddenly, the sound of a guitar riff snaps my attention to the stage as the band launches into their first song.

The Restrictions play for about an hour. Miah finds me in the crowd as he's playing and periodically smiles at me or watches me while he sings. At one point he winks, and just like everything this boy does, it's like magic and makes me feel things in places down below, where I haven't ventured to often in my life.

When the band is done playing, Miah, Lars, and the guitarist, who I haven't met yet, approach us while we are still standing in the group with Evie.

"Ahh, I see you've met the infamous Miss Evie. The baddest bitch in the game," Miah teases with a mocking smile directed at his youngest sister.

"Don't be a jerk in front of Cece, Miah. I've decided she's sweeter than Gram's lemon meringue pie, so don't fucking hurt her, dick!" Evie sneers back with a playful smile. I stand frozen, my eyes as wide as saucers, flicking between the two of them. I feel like I'm missing something each time Evie speaks. Like there's a big secret I don't know about, yet.

"Sorry about her; she has anger issues." Miah laughs and then turns to gesture toward the guitarist. "Hey, Cora, I wanted you to meet Hunter. I wasn't sure if you guys had been introduced yet."

I shake my head no. "We haven't. Nice to meet you, Hunter."

Hunter smiles and waves. I take notice that he stands a few inches shorter than Miah, which is not unusual given that Miah is remarkably tall. His hair is a buzz cut, leaving brown spikes on top of his head. And his olive skin makes his rich-mahogany eyes stand out, accentuated by long black eyelashes.

Man, I wish I had his eyelashes.

"Nice to finally meet you too," he says so softly that it's hard to even hear him. Hunter keeps his broad chin down while he speaks, which makes me think he's shy. A girl quietly joins our circle, coming up alongside Hunter and touching his arm. I watch the way she rubs her hand along his biceps, which draws my attention to how big his arms are—they look like they are going to tear through his sleeves at any moment. The girl hanging on his arm tugs his hand and begins to lead him away from the group. Miah follows suit and takes my hand, ushering me back toward the house.

"You guys sounded great, as per usual," I say, following him through the crowd. "I hate to do this, Miah, but we've got to head home. Taylor's about to lock herself in the bathroom with her face in the toilet if I don't get her out of here soon."

He stops and turns. We are extremely close to each other, which makes me take a fumbling step back. He's looking at me intently. "Cece, I really want to take you on a date. I've been working up the courage to ask you because I was afraid." He's still holding my hand and his thumb is moving in circles over my knuckles. "I've been afraid of your thoughts on the whole age thing. I wasn't sure how you felt about it, and I want to tell you that I respect you, I always will. I want you to know that you never have to feel pressured to do anything or be someone you're not with me." He pauses, and I notice sweat is forming around his hairline. "If we date, if you feel how I do, I want you to know that I don't care what anyone thinks, but I will respect your parents and friends. And I will always respect you." I look down at our hands, and his thumb is still gently caressing my skin.

Before I run through all the worst-case scenarios in my mind, my mouth opens. "Yes, I would really like to date, or go on dates with you." I told myself I would let this be whatever it wanted to be so here I am, doing just that.

※ ※ ※

Taylor sleeps the entire drive back to her mom's place. I have to sling her arm over my shoulder and practically carry her into the house. I lay her on her bed, but she wakes up as soon as her body hits the mattress and she runs to the bathroom. She spends a good half hour throwing up everything she consumed at the party. In the past, I've tried to hold Taylor's hair back and comfort her, but she got really pissed one time because she doesn't want me seeing her like that, so I haven't done it since. While I wait, I change into my pajamas and order us a pizza. It's the same thing every time Taylor drinks: she gets wasted, pukes, and then is back to normal (but super giggly) and ready to devour everything in sight.

She stumbles out of the bathroom and into her room, swapping her party clothes for a baggy T-shirt and sleep shorts. Once she's dressed, she plops down on the bed. "I'm *so* hungry."

"Good thing, because I ordered a giant pizza," I respond.

"I fucking love you, you know that?" she replies, sounding exhausted. I chuckle and lie down on the bed next to her.

"Cora, I want you to know that I won't judge you for dating an older guy. I also want you to know that it's time for you to do what makes you happy. I've watched you for the past whatever years, because I can't count right now, carrying the weight of your parents' marriage on your back.

It's time to let it go and focus on you. Ya know? Like, you do you!" She takes my hand and squeezes it. "What happens to them is not because of you. They both love you so much and they always will. Date him, Cora—he makes you happy. Plus, he's fine. Like . . . like, *super* fine. Like Benji from Good Charlotte fine! Or Joel because they look the same, with the whole twin thing."

"Okay, okay, okay! Just rest your little head until pizza comes." I squeeze her hand back, laughing at her until I can't breathe.

I guess I haven't taken a good look at myself lately to realize I do carry my parents' issues with me everywhere I go. I'm not going to stop myself from dating Miah because I'm afraid of what my parents will think. I need to live my life and snap out of this misery I've been in since their fighting and the divorce. I do know that at some point I will have to help my mom with her drinking problem, but I'm not going to worry about that right now. I want to be with Miah—I want him in so many ways and I'm going to have him in all those ways.

CHAPTER FIVE

In the Car, I Just Can't Wait . . .

Only one more sleep until my first date with Jeremiah. It's been a week since I saw him at his house. He texted me the Sunday after his party, officially asking me to go on a date with him, and of course I said yes.

Taylor and I have been going over all the ways to approach my mom about it. See, I'm not good at lying, but more importantly, I don't *like* to lie. I guess I want to go through life guilt-free. I also feel like when I lie, bad things happen, no matter what. So after all our planning and scheming, we both decide I will just tell my mom I'm going on a date with an older guy and deal with her reaction when it happens.

I'm sitting at the kitchen island eating my usual bowl of cereal before school when my mom enters the room and opens the refrigerator. She grabs a protein shake and an orange and takes a seat next to me at the island. This is odd, because we don't spend many mornings eating together since she's usually out the door before I am.

"Two-hour delay at the elementary school today," she says, before taking a sip of her shake.

"Mmmm," I respond, chewing a mouthful of cereal.

"Your dad found a condo in Biddeford. He called yesterday and asked if he could start to see you some weekends. He suggested you drive down to see him, but I suggested *he* drive up to see *you*. *He* is your father, after all, and the one who ruined *our* lives." She huffs and gulps down more of her shake. Biddeford is about a twenty-five-minute drive from here on a good day, forty-five minutes to an hour on a not-so-good day.

"Ha, yeah . . . I don't know if I want to give up every weekend of my senior year to be in a town where I know no one. He can call me, and we can work something out." This angers me a bit, and that anger gives me the courage to tell her about Miah, or should I say, *ask* her about Miah. I put my spoon down and turn so that I'm facing her. She slowly lowers her bottle to the counter and swallows hard. She knows something is coming.

"Hey, Mom, I don't know how to ask you and I don't want you to freak out because I know what it looks like from a mom's perspective, so can you just go into what I'm about to ask you with an open mind?"

She stares at me through slitted eyes for several seconds before she responds, "Okay, continue." She grabs her drink again and takes another sip.

"When I was at that show a few weekends ago, I met a guy. We've been texting back and forth since then and, well . . . he asked me to go on a date with him tomorrow night," I rush through the last bit, mindlessly playing with a fallen Cheerio on the counter.

"What's so wrong with that? Why do I need to be open-minded? Oh god, Cora, is he a convict?" she says, laughing to herself.

"Um, no, not really." My gaze drops to my lap. "It's just . . . it's just, he—he's older than me." My heart is pounding so hard now that I don't even hear my own words. I look up at her through my lashes to see if I can gauge what her reaction will be. She's sitting completely still, no emotions shown on her face.

"Cora, how old is this boy?" she demands, after what feels like forever.

"Twenty-two," I say quickly and flat out. I turn back to my bowl of cereal and start swirling the leftover milk with my spoon. "Look, I get it. If you don't want this to happen, you can say no. I just really like Jeremiah and I hope you can give him a chance."

My mom places her hand on mine, which is still aimlessly moving the spoon through the milk in the bowl. She gently squeezes, stilling my hand. I look up at her, preparing my heart and my head for the worst.

"Cora, I want to meet this boy. You're a great kid. You've never done anything that would make me doubt you or your life decisions, but I want to get to know him before I let you leave the house with him. Have him pick you up here tomorrow so that I can meet him." She turns and stands, and then faces me. "But Cora, if I don't like this boy, it ain't gonna happen." She clears her throat, grabs her keys, and moves to the front door.

Gripping the doorknob, my mom looks over her shoulder at me, smiling. "Have a good day. And Cece, you should probably think of how to bring this up to your father. I can tell you right now, he won't be happy."

She leaves me sitting at the kitchen island frozen in shock—I'd completely forgotten that I would possibly have to tell him about Miah as well. I'm no daddy's girl, but I am his only girl and only child, so he may be a bit tougher to crack. Just as if my mind manifested this situation, I get a text from Dad.

Great.

It's a question: *Hey, Cora, would you be free to grab dinner with me on Saturday?*

After reading the text, I start mindlessly tapping my fingernails on the counter, debating my response. It's not that I may have to bring up Miah to him since my mom may not even like him . . . I doubt that, though; she will love him. It's the fact that since my dad cheated on my mom and I found out, I just don't feel comfortable around him anymore. I feel like I can't be myself. As if there will always be a huge bubble of emotions and things unsaid between us, and it's threatening to burst at any moment.

I type back: *Sure, the usual? Sea Breeze Diner?*

He instantly replies: *See you at 5.*

I clean up my mess, grab my bag, and head out for school.

* * *

Friday evening finally arrives after the slowest week of my life. Yesterday and today dragged on the most, and I thought they would never end. I'm standing in front of my full-length mirror holding up two dresses in front of me. I've narrowed down my decision to either black with white polka dots or black with small white flowers. After debating for a while, I toss the polka dots back in my closet and decide on the flowers. Miah will be here in twenty minutes to pick me up and, more importantly, to meet my mom. I'm so nervous that I keep needing to blot the sweat on my upper lip and forehead every ten minutes. I'm waiting until the last second to put on my dress so that I don't sweat through it. I make my way across my bedroom and turn off my stereo system that's been playing Blink-182 on repeat for almost two hours straight while I got ready. I throw on the dress and my black slip-on Vans. Once more, I do a sweat dab, check myself in the mirror, and head downstairs to wait for Miah.

When I enter the kitchen, my mom is sitting at the island. She's drinking a glass of red wine and mindlessly flipping through a trashy magazine (which is my name for her stupid celebrity gossip tabloids). When she hears me enter the room, she looks up over her reading glasses that are sitting on the bridge of her nose.

"Well, you look very nice," she comments with a smile as she takes a sip of her wine.

"Thanks, Ma, but please don't make me any more nervous or make me doubt this dress. I can't do another outfit change, or the sweat will only intensify." I begin fanning my armpits when I hear a car coming up the driveway.

"Shit! He's early!" I grab a water from the fridge and chug half the bottle in an attempt to cool my internal temperature.

"Calm down, Cora. Jeez, you would think this boy is God himself with the way you are acting." She stands up and tosses her trashy magazine, well, in the trash.

The doorbell rings and I spring on my toes to head toward the door. I take a deep breath and quietly mutter "you can do this, you got this," then I pull the door open. Miah is standing in front of me with a bouquet of tie-dyed roses and a smirk on his face. He's wearing black fitted jeans and a black short-sleeve polo shirt that shows off his sleeve and hand tattoos. He's so tall that I have to crane my neck to look up at him. His polo shirt is tight across his chest and around his biceps, and his jeans are snug on his thighs, fitting him perfectly. He's not super muscular, but he definitely likes to do some sort of exercise that gives him a toned physique.

"For me?" I say by way of greeting as he presents the flowers.

"For you."

I grab the bouquet and step back as he walks inside. He leans in and hugs me. His warm body engulfs me, and his scent is mesmerizing. That warm feeling is activated low in my belly, and butterflies swarm my stomach. I push the feelings aside quickly as I hear my mom clear her throat behind me. I quickly step away from Miah and turn toward the noise. My mom is standing a few feet from us, watching with her arms crossed and her reading glasses now resting up on her head.

Miah moves toward her with his hand out. "Mrs. Mitchell, I'm Jeremiah Novak."

My mom takes his hand into hers as she smiles at him with a bit of hesitation. "Jeremiah, nice to meet you. Cora has told me a lot about you, but I understand there's quite an age difference between the two of you. Tell me, Jeremiah, do you drink or do drugs?" One eyebrow is perched up on her forehead as she waits for his answer. I'm sure she's thinking he's going to say, *"Yes, what twenty-two-year-old doesn't?"*

Well, Jeremiah Novak doesn't, and Lucy is about to find out.

Miah chuckles nervously before he answers. "Actually, no. I don't like the way either makes me feel and um . . . well, after my mom passed away, my dad became an alcoholic, so it's something I stay away from." My mom and I are staring at him with our mouths slightly open at his response, both of us are unsure how to respond.

Why didn't he tell me this before when I asked why he doesn't drink? Maybe it was the wrong place, wrong time?

Maybe someday he will bring it up to me, but I won't ever pressure him to talk about it.

I turn and head toward the sink to put my flowers in a vase with some water. As I leave the two of them by the door, I see my mom give her head a quick little shake before she responds to Miah. "I'm so sorry about your mother, and your father as well. That must have been very difficult for you."

"Thank you, Mrs. Mitchell. I really lost two parents when my mom passed, but my dad's recovering, so it's been great to have him back in my life," Miah responds with a quick nod. My mom clicks her tongue softly with a guilty look on her face.

When I'm done with the flowers, I return to Miah's side.

"Have her home by twelve o'clock, no later, or this won't happen again," my mom decrees, waggling her pointer finger between us.

"Yes, ma'am. I will return her home safe and at eleven fifty-five."

"Okaaaayyy! Well, that was fun. Time to go. See you later, Mom," I say, opening the door and pushing Miah through it.

"Cora, best behavior, please!" I hear her shout as I close the door.

Walking down the driveway, I can see Miah's car. It's a new black BMW that has tinted windows, fancy rims, and, bolted above the Maine license plate, a customized European plate that reads "BEAMER 0612." In a weird way, his car looks like him. Sleek, outfitted in all black, and with stickers on the back like it too has tattoos.

Miah and I get into the car. I slide onto the cold leather seat and nearly fall backward because of how low his car is. He fumbles with the radio a bit and then looks at me.

"What do you want to listen to? You pick, I'll drive." He hands me a white iPod and I begin to scan through the bands. I land on Reel Big Fish and play "Everything Sucks." Miah starts laughing as he's looking over his shoulder, backing down the driveway.

"I'm sorry, I can change it!" I grab the iPod again. He's putting the car into first gear but stops and places his hand on mine, which stops me from changing the song.

"No, I'm laughing because I was listening to Reel Big Fish on my way here. I like to listen to them when I'm in a really good mood. Good choice." He moves his hand back onto the gear shift and starts driving.

"So . . . what are our plans tonight, Mr. Novak?" I ask, watching his face as he concentrates on driving.

"Well, Little Jetta, you should know by now I'm an unconventional guy, and although I love a good meal at Olive Garden, that will not be my plan for tonight."

"Are you going to share your plans or is it a secret?" I prod as I tap my pointer finger on my chin.

"Not a secret, I'm no good at secrets. I planned on grabbing some takeout from Golden Wok—I hope you like Chinese food." He turns his head to me abruptly with worry written all over his face, as though he hadn't even thought of the possibility that I might not like Chinese food.

"I love Golden Wok. Their crab rangoons are my weakness."

"Good, good. And then I want to take you to one of my favorite spots in the city. It's sort of like a picnic, I guess," he says, shrugging his shoulders to his ears.

"That sounds perfect," I nod reassuringly.

* * *

Miah carries our Golden Wok order in a brown paper bag, and I follow close behind him. I watch as his feet balance on rocks and exposed tree roots along a tiny dirt pathway that looks to be worn down from the regulars who know what's hidden at the end of the trail. The sky isn't dark yet, so it's easy for us to make our way down the sloped, narrow footpath heading toward a spot near the Fore River. We trek for about five minutes before he stops at the edge of a small clearing. Standing next to him, I see a large granite statue of a whale, and a small park bench sits in front of it.

"Is this okay?" Miah asks, holding out his hand to the bench.

"Perfect, I'm starving!" I take a seat on the bench. Miah unbags our food and hands me my container of noodles with chopsticks and a plastic fork.

"How did you find this place?" I ask, dipping my chopsticks into my noodles. Miah eases into the space next to me on the bench with his noodles in one hand, and he places the crab rangoons between us.

"Eh, I like to skateboard around the city a lot and find secret places where I can hide out. This is my favorite find. I feel like I can seclude myself away from the world out here."

My heart stutters a bit when I realize that he has taken me to a place that means something to him and I'm probably one of the few people he's shared this with.

"I really like it here. I wish I had the courage to explore by myself. I get bad anxiety about doing things alone. It's weird, and it's a work in progress that I hope to overcome someday."

"I get that. I have anxiety too. At the end of the day, we're only human. No one is perfect, Cece," Miah says before shoving a crab rangoon in his mouth.

"I'm really sorry to hear about your mom and your dad, Miah. I can't imagine what you went through. I feel like this stupid little girl because my life-altering crisis for the past few years has been my parents arguing too much and getting a divorce. It's just, when you think you have it bad, you really don't have it *that* bad."

Miah shakes his head while he finishes chewing a second crab rangoon. He sits silently for a second and then responds. "Cora, your parents going through a divorce is hard as well. It's not as though your parents have passed away, but their relationship has died and the memories you had of them together died too. You're grieving a loss, so please don't think you're a stupid little girl. Your feelings are valid, and I'm sorry you're going through this." He turns his head and stares right into my eyes. We both don't say anything for a moment, and in that moment, looking into his eyes, time seems to slip from me and my heart feels less heavy.

I want to kiss him so badly.

I break eye contact when the thought of kissing him pops into my mind. I blush and shift my gaze toward the to-go container that's warming my lap. Miah and I sit in silence, both of us eating our noodles slowly. After a little while, I open my mouth to tell him that my mom has a slight drinking problem, but I close it quickly, thinking I'd better not. I know my mom is a borderline alcoholic, but I realize I don't feel comfortable disclosing that to Miah just yet. Especially since it's the first time I'm hearing his dad is a recovering alcoholic.

I break the silence first. "Thank you for this, this is really nice."

"If I can be honest, Cece, I hope this isn't our last date," he responds.

Having eaten our fill, Miah closes up the takeout containers and packs what's left of his food back into the paper bag. I close my container and start to place it in the bag when Miah gently takes it from me. "Please, let me," he says with a smile.

"If *I* can be honest, this is very scary to me. I feel like you are so much wiser than me," I chuckle nervously.

"Really I'm not, I'm just a good actor. I'm scared too, but only because I really like you." Miah taps his elbow to mine and then stands up. He reaches his hand out to me and I take it as he grabs the bag of food with his other hand. We begin our journey back to Miah's car and he holds my hand the entire time. When we reach his car, he opens the passenger side door, I slide in, and he closes the door behind me. I watch Miah hustle around the front of the car to the driver's side and get in.

"Where to now, Mr. Novak?" I ask.

"Well, I was thinking maybe ice cream, and then head back to your place?" Miah asks as he starts the engine.

"I love ice cream, but can we skip my place? My mom tends to go out with the girls on the weekend, and sometimes they end up back at our house. I'm not in the mood for dealing with a bunch of drunk women." I'm fidgeting with the hem of my dress, avoiding his stare. I just know she will be alone and drunk.

Miah laughs a little, "Yeah, that's fine. Are you comfortable with my house, then?" I'm still playing with the hem of my dress, but when his words register, I stop fidgeting and look up at him.

"Of course. Only if you promise me that you still aren't a murderer like in *Texas Chainsaw Massacre*."

Miah shakes his head and laughs. He throws the car into first gear and begins driving, "Nope," he says, popping the *p*.

Miah orders a chocolate, coffee, and cookies 'n' cream milkshake from Mr. Scoops Ice Cream. It sounds amazing, so I get one too. It's a quick drive from Mr. Scoops to Jeremiah's. I forgot how convenient the location of Miah's house is, being that it's downtown. He's close to everything, which is the opposite of where I live on the outskirts of downtown. I'm thankful we decided on his place, because less time driving means more time to spend close to one another.

We are sitting on the couch in the living room, drinking our milkshakes and watching *Mallrats*. It's one of my favorite movies, and I was shocked his roommate owned it but Miah had never seen it. I made him put it on for us and he agreed without any argument.

Thirty minutes into the film, he turns to me, "So . . . what's your life like, Cora? Tell me, what's your favorite color? Favorite band? I'm intrigued to know more about you. I have a feeling you have a very quirky sense of humor, given that this is a favorite movie of yours." Miah is looking down at me, since somehow, in that half hour, we have slumped into each other. I look up at him and butterflies start flying again in my stomach and down further. He's so close that I breathe in the scent of him—slowly so that he can't hear me . . . I don't want to seem like a creep, but I find comfort in the way he smells. The combination of sandalwood, Red Bull, and clean laundry trickles in through my nose and lands heavily in my lower belly. I want to lean in closer and push my lips to his to taste him, but my brain turns on again and tells me not to.

Why do I have a brain again?

I lick my lips, and Miah's eyes catch the movement. He flicks his gaze back to mine and smiles but doesn't move. I'm not even sure he's breathing, he's so still. But then his warm breath brushes my lips . . .

"Purple," I blurt out as I turn my head back toward the TV. "My favorite color, it's purple. My favorite band is Blink-182, with Paramore following close behind. I hate olives and mushrooms, and my favorite food is anything sweet. I love desserts, pastries, and ice cream." I look at him again and my cheeks feel hot. I know they are red. He's still studying me when I gaze back up at him. "What about you?" I ask.

"My favorite color is pink because real men like pink. My favorite band is hard to pick because I like so many, but I would have to say Alkaline Trio. I also don't like olives or mushrooms, so yay for our future pizzas . . . and my favorite food is pizza. If you say you don't like pizza, I will ask you to leave," he jokes.

My eyes are still fixed on him, and I smile. "I love pizza. I'm not a psychopath," I assert with my best eye roll.

My phone buzzes and I grab it from the armrest of the couch. It's Taylor texting me: *Call me when you get home. I need the DEETZ!* I flip my phone closed, knowing I would call her as soon as Miah dropped me off. I check the time on my phone screen and realize it's already 11:30 p.m.

"I hate to break the news, but I should probably get home so that Lucy lets me see you again," I say, beginning to stand up.

"Yeah, absolutely." Miah slowly rises from the couch and gently takes my cup from me.

Before he can get by me, I pivot, abruptly stopping him from passing me. I look up at him. My mind goes blank as I see him staring down at me. His face is inches away from mine, and I can't hold back any longer. I lean into Miah, stretching up on my toes, and lightly touch my lips to his. The warmth from his lips seeps into mine, traveling to my heart and then further into my body. A heat settles snuggly at the bottom of my stomach, burning and turning into need. I immediately pull away because I notice he's not leaning into the kiss as much as I had hoped.

"I'm sorry, I just—I wanted to feel your lips on mine," I stammer, taking a step back and rubbing my thumb over my bottom lip. Miah doesn't move. In fact, he doesn't say anything at all.

I put my back to him and start to walk out of the room when Miah finally responds, halting me. "Cora, wait. I'm sorry, I'm just honestly shocked. I had every intention of kissing you . . . I just was going to ask you first. I never expected you to beat me to it." I slowly turn on my heels until I'm facing him again, but I don't verbally respond. After several seconds of us examining one another, Miah begins striding toward me, but he brushes past. I turn my head to watch him walk into the kitchen, but keep my feet planted in place. Once he's gone, I direct my gaze down to my dirty black-and-white checkered vans as I think of what to say or do next.

Seriously, dude? Like, do you respect me that *much that you won't even kiss me back? I think it's obvious my answer would have been yes, I want you to kiss me, considering my actions. This is a waste of time.*

Just as I spin to hustle my way out of the house, hoping to run out the front door and leave my embarrassment and anger behind . . . I find Miah standing in the archway separating the kitchen and the living room, leaning on the frame and watching me. Before either one of us can speak, he abruptly closes the distance between us in two quick steps. He gently takes hold of my hair in his hand, and he pulls me in closer with the other. His mouth crashes into mine and I can't help but smile and let out a small giggle. This time when our lips touch, it's intense, and it's deeper and desperate.

My tongue grazes lazily along Miah's bottom lip, and his

tongue responds to mine. I press into him farther, and my whole body is tingling and hot and in need of being closer to him. I lift my hands to his hair, playing with the strands and running them through my fingers. He stops and I softly bite his bottom lip. We stay inches apart, breathing into one another, and I swear he's breathing life and feelings and everything I've been so numb to back into me.

He pulls away and a smirk tugs at the corners of his mouth. "I had to throw those fucking cups away to kiss you properly." He grabs my hands as he leans in to place a soft peck on my lips, and my body blooms again, aching for more, but I let him break the kiss. "Little Jetta, I hope we can do that again. If you'll let me?" He winks at me. My body is on the fritz. I've never felt this way before, and I don't know if this is normal. Miah's placed a hunger inside me and he's the only meal I need to end this starvation.

"It definitely will not be the last time," I say, squeezing his hands.

CHAPTER SIX

Wine and Dine

It's been raining and chilly all day. The weather has begun to make its way into the raw, wet season of fall, but I have a smile on my face as I replay moments from last night with Miah in my mind.

I'm driving through the drizzle on my way to meet my dad at the Sea Breeze Diner, which is a regular spot of ours. We would frequent the diner on Saturday nights when we were craving breakfast for dinner, just my dad and me. My mom has never been a fan of breakfast. She often says the smell of maple syrup makes her want to throw up—apparently she had a bad experience with syrup when she was younger. So Dad and I made it our thing. We would stuff ourselves silly with pancakes and bacon and talk about happenings in our lives or he would tell me stories about his childhood. It was fun, and I always looked forward to it. We haven't done this in about two years.

I park directly in front of the diner, that way I won't get wet on my way in. I can see my dad through the window, in the booth next to the door. In my best effort to avoid the now-giant raindrops, I make a mad dash for the entrance, jog up the steps, and open the door. As I shuffle inside, I briefly check my clothes to see how wet I got from the rain. I notice the restaurant is not as noisy as it usually is, and looking around, I confirm there aren't many people here tonight. The air smells of coffee and syrup, which is comforting to me. For a moment, it brings me back to my childhood and the fun times my dad and I shared here.

The high I was feeling from my date last night washes out of me like the rain falling outside as I take the handful of steps to my dad's table. When I slide into the red booth and sit down across from him, he looks up from his menu. "Hey, Daughter," he greets with a meek smile.

"Hey, Dad," I say, unenthusiastically. I break eye contact quickly to study the menu. I already know what I'm ordering, so there's no point in reading the menu, but I can't seem to meet his eyes. Not when we still have the invisible bubble of tension between us. I spare a glance up at him through my eyelashes, keeping my head down so as to not make it obvious that I'm looking at him. He doesn't notice because he's reading his menu again.

My dad looks up again and notices me observing him. "What are we thinking, little girl?" he asks.

It breaks my heart the way he still calls me his little girl. It's a term of endearment he uses when he's proud. I'm sad because I always felt safe with my dad growing up. He was always my safe haven, but now when I look at him, I don't even know who I'm looking at. This isn't the dad I once knew; he and my mom were so in love . . . or so I thought. He was the guy who was always around, coached my little league team, took me clothes shopping for school. Once, my dad even picked me up from school when the nurse called to let him know I had had my first-ever period-related incident and that I refused to leave the bathroom. He showed up and comforted me, reassuring me that it was totally normal and that it happens more often than I know. He then took me to get a new pair of pants and we spent the rest of the day together. Now, I'm looking across the table at a sad man who knows he made a mistake but it's too late. My mom and I are beyond the point of apologies and his useless attempts to act like everything's normal and okay. How will we ever get past this?

"I guess I'm thinking . . . Why? Why did you do this to us?" I don't know where this is coming from, the courage to ask him, but it slipped out and there is no shoving it back in my mouth now. He's staring at me, eyes wide and in shock. I guess he had no idea how much I knew. Before he can respond, the waitress approaches, asking us if we are ready to order.

"I'll take a turkey club and a water, please. White bread and mayo. Thanks," I say, handing the waitress my menu. My dad's eyes are still locked on me.

"Sir?" the waitress presses, waiting for his order.

"Uh, oh yeah, my turn. I'll get the eggs benedict, please. Bacon, and a side of white toast," my dad finally stutters out. He gives his menu to the waitress and waits for her to walk away. "Cora, I'm not sure what your mother has told you about us, and I know we need to talk about it, but I just don't think here is the right place," he forces out sternly.

"Okay, well when would be a good time, Dad? Because I watched you pack up your shit and walk out of our family home like you were going on a business trip. Like it was no big deal that you were leaving your entire life behind in that home, including me, your daughter. We can keep playing this stupid fucking game, all three of us, where we pretend that I'm still a child and I had no idea what you both were screaming about night after night. Acting like I'm safe and sound sleeping in my bed in my make-believe soundproof room."

"Cora, language. Don't speak to me like that, I'm still your father," he snaps back, his face turning bright red.

My hands are shaking from how angry I've become. I just want the truth from him, but I'm betting I won't get it anytime soon. I calm myself down as we sit in silence. Our waitress delivers our food, and we begin to eat while the tension between us builds.

By the time the check comes, my dad finally breaks the ice. "Well, thanks for grabbing dinner with me."

I don't respond. I just keep my face and gaze toward the window.

When he realizes that I don't intend on responding, he continues. "I wanted to let you know that I got a condo in Biddeford, and I would like to start having you come down a couple of weekends a month and stay the night with me. I spoke about it with your mom, and she said to run it by you."

"Yeah, I can't promise you anything. It's my senior year and I really want to be here with Taylor and go to more happenings around town before I graduate. I'm also seeing someone, so I would really like to keep my weekends open."

His eyebrows perk up on his forehead at the mention of me seeing someone. "Oh, I didn't know. Well, I would like to meet him or her."

"Dad, seriously?!" I say, rolling my eyes.

"Cece, I'm just trying to be open and let you know that I accept you the way you are, and I always will." This is something I've always known about my dad. He didn't have to tell me, but I know he won't accept the fact that I'm dating an older guy. I'm not brave enough to take on that whole argument tonight.

"Dad, when I'm ready, you will meet him, but it's still very new." He nods at my response. I know that I'm safe from the Miah conversation . . . for now.

"You let me know when you can come see me at my new place, and we can do a movie night. We can also chat about what's happening in our lives too, not just between your mom and me but maybe about school, friends, and this new guy?"

Now it's my turn to nod.

We finish up at the table and leave the restaurant. My dad walks me to my car and does a quick inspection of my Jetta to make sure everything is running efficiently and safely. When he's done, we give each other small hugs and I jump in my car and drive off without looking back at him.

As I'm driving home from the diner, my phone keeps going off. I try not to check my phone while driving, but I never get this many texts or calls at once. I lean over to the passenger seat, digging my right hand deep into my purse, and pull out my phone. I briefly look down at it when I come to a stoplight and see that it's Taylor. Then it dawns on me: I was so dazed from my amazing date with Miah last night that I never called to tell her about it. She's probably pissed. I put my phone in my cup holder and plan to deal with it when

I get home . . . until it starts ringing again.

I grab it, frustrated, and answer, "Taylor, what in the world—"

"Cora, no time to yell at me," Taylor says, cutting me off. "You need to come straight home. I just ran into your mom at Cal's and she was so drunk she threw up all over the floor. I'm at your house with her now. I got her cleaned up and in bed."

"Be there in ten." I slam the phone shut and toss it back in the cup holder.

I pull into the driveway in less than ten minutes—it's usually a twenty-minute drive. When I get inside, I run up to my mom's room and find her passed out in her bed with Taylor sitting next to her, back against the headboard, texting away.

"What the fuck happened?" I ask, shocked.

"Cece, your mom is getting bad. She was out with the girls again and they started doing shots and she just kept going. I overheard one of the women say that she has a source that has seen your dad out and about with that chick he was cheating on your mom with. I hate to tell you that, Cece, but I gotta let you know, these 'girls' are not her friends."

I sit quietly at the foot of the bed just looking at my mom. My heart is breaking for her. I'm embarrassed for her and myself, and I'm sad and angry for her. I love my mom, and she's done everything for me since I can remember. She deserves so much better than this.

"Taylor, I'm going to need help getting her help. I don't think she's an alcoholic, but I'm afraid that she's rapidly going down that path. Will you help me?" My voice is breaking.

Taylor grabs my hand and looks me dead in the eyes. "I am your best friend. You don't need to ask me for help because I'm going to be here with you whether you want me to be or not." She gives me a small smile and squeezes my hand.

"I love you, Taylor. I mean it, I would be lost without you." I squeeze her hand back while I look at her. I truly mean it. She's my best friend and my sister. Without her, I would have no one. "What should we do?"

"You've gotta confront this head-on, Cece. I can be there with you to tell her how bad tonight really was. Maybe that will make her want to change her ways, if an outsider is telling her what her behavior looked like?"

Just as Taylor finishes, my phone goes off. I pop it open and see a text from Miah: *Hey, everything all right? We haven't spoken all day and well, I hate to do this, but Lars said Taylor had an emergency with your mom at Cal's? I was worried about you.*

"Shit!" I whisper.

"What's wrong?" Taylor asks. I pass her my phone with Miah's text. She reads it quickly and hands me my phone back.

"Cece, it's fine. Just tell him it was an issue with your mom and you're okay. When you're ready, talk to him about her. I don't think he's going to pressure you into anything."

"You're right."

I type out my reply: *I'm so sorry. I had dinner with my dad tonight and yes, there was an emergency with my mom, but it's all good. I hope you had a good day. Call you tomorrow?*

It doesn't take long for his response to come through: *Oh good! I was hoping my kiss didn't scare you off . . . I've been thinking about you all day and how I can't wait to see you again. Talk tomorrow for sure. Sweet dreams, Little Jetta.*

I read his text and smile, pulling my phone to my chest. I glance over at Taylor and she's looking at me like I've gone crazy. Giving her a playful scowl, I close my phone and stand up. I check my mom and tuck her in, then I start making my way to my bedroom as Taylor follows behind.

"Want to stay the night? We can catch up on what happened with Miah and me last night," I say, still smiling stupidly.

Taylor lightly slaps my arm. "Shut up! What happened and why didn't you tell me sooner?"

We enter my room and I jump on the bed, patting the spot next to me. "Stay with me, let's chat." Without hesitation, Taylor leaps onto the bed and gets comfortable next to me. Both of us giggling, I immediately start going over every detail of my date with Miah . . . and that kiss. We also talk about how Lars makes Taylor feel and how they are *officially* official now. She's super happy with him, and he even comes and watches her field hockey games—which reminds me that I should make it to a game soon too.

I periodically check on my mom until Taylor and I doze off around two in the morning. I left my bedroom door open to make sure I could hear my mom call if she needed me. At one point, I heard her heavy footsteps on the wooden stairs, a kitchen cabinet slam shut, followed by the sound of running water. I assumed she was getting herself a glass of water and that she was feeling well enough to walk around.

The sound of my phone ringing stirs me from sleep on Sunday. I grab it off my nightstand and see it's Miah. I shoot upright, quickly clearing my throat as I flip open my phone.

"Hey," I say groggily.

"Hey, I'm sorry! Did I wake you?" Miah responds.

"No, yes—but it's okay!" I reassure him.

"Well, you sound super cute when you're tired," Miah says with a slight chuckle. "Listen, I was calling to see if you wanted to hang out today. I could pick you up around two and we could have some fun?"

"Ummmmm, yeah, actually. That would be great. I have some homework and things to do this morning, so this afternoon works."

"Great! I'll see you later then. I can't wait," Miah says, and we both hang up.

I notice Taylor is not sleeping next to me anymore, so I roll out of bed and decide to head downstairs. On my way down, I also decide that if my mom is up, it's time to talk to her about her behavior lately and her drinking habits.

When I get to the kitchen, Taylor is sitting at the island eating a bowl of cereal next to my mom, who's reading the newspaper with her breakfast smoothie in front of her. My mom turns and watches me get my cereal.

"Hey, Cece," Taylor greets me. "Sorry, I couldn't sleep, so I came down early to get something to eat. I was starving."

"Eh, no big deal. Jeremiah called and he's picking me up at two and we are hanging out for the day," I announce. Taylor's smile is beaming but my mom is eyeing me over her newspaper, through the top of her reading glasses that are sitting on the bridge of her nose. I can already tell she's about to snap at the fact that I didn't ask her, but after last night, I don't really care what she has to say.

"What?" I say, looking at my mom. Taylor's smile drops as she stands and makes her way to the sink.

"You never asked me if this was okay," my mom says, closing the newspaper and placing it on the island in front of her.

"Listen, Mom, after last night, I don't think I need to ask you permission to live my life since I'm more of the adult in this house than you are," I fire back, slamming the carton of milk on the counter. I turn to face her, and my heart is beating so fast, my temper is increasing by the second. She continues to look at me through her glasses as her face flushes red.

"Cora, now is not the time to talk about this in front of Taylor."

"No, you know what, Lucy? Taylor can stay and listen, considering she's the one who saved you last night." Taylor walks back to her seat next to my mom at the kitchen island. My best friend looks like a deer in headlights, her eyes are so big. I can tell she's uncomfortable, but she promised she would do this with me.

My mom takes off her glasses and places them on the table next to the newspaper. She's shaking her head from side to side. "Cora, I'm going through a really hard time right now and I don't need this."

"Stop right there!" I shout at her, walking closer to the island. "I'm going through a hard time too, but I haven't been acting out or drowning my sorrows in drugs or alcohol. I'm still a child under your roof, going to school and struggling with her parents' divorce. I still need a mom and a dad, regardless of what they are going through." My fists are clenched at my sides, and I can tell my mom is shocked by how I'm acting. "You embarrassed me last night in front of my friends and, worse, you embarrassed yourself in front of your 'friends,'" I say, using air quotes. "Your drinking has gotten out of control over the past two years. I'm telling you right now that you need to get it under control. If you don't, I'm leaving this house and living on my own, and I don't give a fuck what you or dad says." I'm shouting at her and I don't mean to be, but I'm so angry that I have to be the adult for the both of them. I'm sick of being the only person who cares enough to do something, and I'm sick of being the only person in this family who's keeping it together. Whatever "keeping it together" means at this point.

"Cora, listen, last night wasn't that bad. I don't know why you are so bent out of shape about it," my mom calmly responds.

I look over at Taylor, who's looking at my mom with a pained expression on her face. "Um, actually, Lucy, it was pretty bad. Cal threatened to call the police to escort you home since you couldn't stand on your own. My boyfriend had to drive you here and put you to bed. While I waited with you for Cora to get home, you threw up about four times. It was only seven o'clock when this all happened."

There's a lingering silence in the air while Taylor and I wait for my mom to respond. She turns in her chair and stands, making her way over to the sink. She washes out her glass that had her smoothie in it. When she's done, she turns back to us.

"I'm sorry for everything that is happening right now, Cora. What do you want me to do?"

"Mom, you need to stop drinking. It's gone too far, and I won't deal with it anymore," I say immediately.

My mom moves closer and stops in front of me, resting her hands on the sides of my arms, giving me a light squeeze. "Okay. I can do that. I'm going to need some help, though, but I can do it."

"First, you need to stop going out with the girls. They aren't your friends and are a bad influence. I'm here to help you with whatever you need, Mom, but you need new friends and hobbies."

She nods at my response. "Yes . . . yeah, I agree. Starting today, I'm changing."

CHAPTER SEVEN

Pink for Claire

When Miah picks me up to hang out, I'm still feeling upset over what happened with my mom last night and our argument this morning. Miah is driving and I've been silently looking out the window. I'm so lost in my thoughts that I don't even think to ask where we are going. It's just nice not to have to be alone right now.

"Hey, Little Jetta, everything all right?" Miah asks. He grabs my hand and squeezes it. "You seem deep in thought today and unusually quiet."

I continue to stay silent as I wonder how to tell Miah about my mom. There's no comfortable way to explain it, so I just start. "Erm, no . . . ," I hesitate a bit, building up my confidence until I can go on. "There's something I need to tell you, but I've been afraid to and I'm trying to figure out how to bring it up." I sigh, looking at him. I hold his hand in mine as I mindlessly rub his knuckles with my thumb.

Taking a deep breath, I continue. "Miah, my mom's a heavy drinker. She has been for the past two years, ever since my dad lost his job, and it's gotten worse recently." Miah's expression hasn't changed since I started speaking. He still looks calm, but I can see a slight sadness on his face. "I've been too scared to say anything since I found out your dad is a recovering alcoholic. I didn't want to unload my issues on you so soon into our relationship. I also didn't want you to think I came with so much baggage."

He suddenly pulls into a parking lot and shifts his car into park. Taking both my hands in his, he abruptly turns to face me. "Cora, first, you can tell me anything you want to. I really like you, and I'm not running off anytime soon. Second, that's not your baggage, so don't carry it around like it is. I used to think I was the reason for my dad's drinking, but one day I realized I'm not. That's not on me, and it's not on my mom nor my sisters. I've been through this before, and maybe in some weird way, we were meant to meet each other so that I can help you through this." He tilts his head slightly, thinking for a moment. "My sisters and I had each other, but I can't imagine not having any siblings to go through this with. So I'm here for you, Cora. I will do anything you need me to do. You are not alone."

I try not to cry, but my eyes sting and I can feel the tears collecting and brimming on my bottom lids. One falls just as Miah leans in and kisses me. It's a passionate yet gentle kiss that I lean into because my heart feels like it's healing with each moment that passes of his lips on mine. When he breaks the kiss, he holds my face in his hands and his thumbs gently wipe away the tears that are now freely falling.

I grab his wrists and look into his eyes. "Thank you, Miah. It feels so good to hear someone tell me I'm not alone. I've been feeling so stuck in my own head lately. I have Taylor, but I feel like I unload way too much onto her sometimes."

I smirk at him, and he smirks back. But his turns to a slight grimace when he says, "Lars told me what happened last night with your mom, but I didn't want to pry. I wanted you to tell me yourself when or if you felt comfortable enough."

"Yeah, it was pretty embarrassing." I loose another heavy sigh. "I spoke to her this morning about getting help and she said she would, but I feel like I will need to initiate the help and get the ball rolling for her. She's devastated by the divorce. My dad's just gone. Rumor has it he's still seeing the mystery woman he cheated with . . ." Shaking my head to clear away the thought, I announce as perkily as I can, "Anyway, I just want to enjoy today and forget about it. Is that all right with you?"

"Absolutely. If you want, I can give you the information for the treatment program my dad did and the therapist my sisters and I took him to where we did family sessions. It helped him to see how his behavior was affecting all of us." Miah takes out his phone and asks for my email address, typing away as I tell him. He snaps his phone closed and shoves it back into his front pocket. He looks over at me again with an empathetic smile.

"Thank you, Miah. That's all I really know what to say right now." I'm truly at a loss for words.

Jarring me from my thoughts, I hear his car door open and see him jump out. He walks around to my door, opens it, and holds out his hand. I take it and climb out.

"Where are we?" I ask, looking up at him.

"My favorite store in the whole world. Hi-Fi Records!" He says with an eager expression on his face. I start laughing at him, but I'm genuinely excited to browse the record store. I love finding new bands and adding CDs to my collection.

When we walk in, the guy behind the counter looks up and recognizes Miah. "Heyyyy, Miah! Good to see you, man. It's been a few weeks—was starting to get worried about you." He's short and older looking, with long, dark hair that's graying and wrinkles around his eyes when he smiles.

"Yo, Joe! I've been busy with work and band practice," Miah says to him, walking over to the first row of records by the door. "Got anything new?"

"Ah yes, busy living life. I got a few new in, like a perfectly used Madness album you would enjoy. *One Step Beyond*, it's called. I've also got a Beastie Boys *Licensed to Ill* that I know you would like too."

"Joe, that is just what I want to hear!" Miah enthusiastically responds.

I follow his lead through the rows of new and used vinyl records, and then I eventually venture off on my own to browse the CDs. We spend a good hour poking around the store until my stomach starts growling. With how tense and awkward it felt at my house after breakfast, I stayed in my room doing homework until Miah picked me up. I didn't even realize I'd skipped lunch, but now I'm trying to keep the grumbling to a minimum. It's no use, and Miah hears my stomach when we are standing at the checkout. He looks over, smiles at me, and winks. "Food was next on the agenda," he says as he grabs his bag of vinyls and the CDs he insisted on buying for me off the counter.

As we leave the record store, we decide to have an early dinner at Olive Garden. And on the drive to the restaurant, we both confess to each other that it's our guilty pleasure... I mean, the chicken alfredo just hits the spot every time. Miah admits that he is obsessed with their lasagna.

We spend most of our dinner talking a lot about my parents' split and how I think it's all going to play out. I'm not too worried about what will happen because I will be in college or moved out by the time they are officially divorced. I tell Miah the story about the letter my dad's work received and how he's still seeing his "secret mistress," but I have yet to meet her. We talk more about my mom's drinking problem and how Taylor is also helping me navigate this mess. There's a lull in the conversation when the food arrives, since we are too busy devouring our meals. As I've nearly managed to stuff myself completely with chicken alfredo, I have the urge to ask Miah about his mom, so I do.

"Miah, can I ask you a question?" I say, looking at him nervously.

He nods his head yes while he chews on a bite of lasagna. He wipes his face with his napkin before he speaks. "Ask away."

There's a moment of silence before I get the courage to pose my question. I exhale a shaky breath. "What was your mom like?" I blurt out.

He swallows another forkful and starts to aimlessly play with the food on his plate, and I follow suit as I wait for his response. I start to get uneasy with the silence, deciding that I asked the wrong question or thinking maybe I'm prying too much since he barely knows me.

"I'm sorry. You don't have to answer that," I say, shaking my head back and forth as I carefully push my plate away.

"No, no, I want to. It's just, it still hurts when I think about her. She was such a kind and gentle soul. She was honestly loved by so many people, especially us, her family. I wish you could have met her. Your aura is very similar to hers. She also felt so safe and calming to be around, and you do too." He's got a large smile on his face now.

Miah takes a moment, and when he continues, he's looking out the restaurant window. "My mom's name was Claire . . . She was diagnosed with breast cancer when I was fourteen. Evie was ten and my other sister, Angie, was twelve. It was extremely difficult for my sisters since they didn't fully understand what was happening, but my mom did a good job putting on a smile every day, even if she had treatment that day or a doctor's appointment. She did her best to keep us happy and maintain a semi-normal life for us. My dad was obviously devastated—my mom was the love of his life. Soulmates, they used to call each other. He didn't turn to drinking until she passed, then it went downhill from there, for him and us kids."

He looks at me while he takes a sip of his drink. I say nothing, wanting him to keep sharing. He puts his glass down and continues. "The doctors were so sure that chemo would work and my mom would be cancer-free in a year or so, but three days before my fifteenth birthday, she went in for bloodwork and they found that the cancer had spread throughout her body. They said she didn't have much time left. She lived for another six months, and in those six months, she took us kids to do everything she possibly could. We went to waterparks, Disney World, we ate ice cream for breakfast, bought a dog and named him Jingles, had the best Halloween costumes ever that year, and she let us eat a ton of candy that night. She took us on a lot of day trips to local places, and we also went to see a lot of movies. I mean, she took us to do *everything*, and we loved every minute of it. It was almost as if we had forgotten she was sick . . . But she started to become very frail and she had a hard time walking, so the trips slowed down. When November came around, she was in a wheelchair, and reality hit us that we were losing our mom." He starts playing with the food on his plate again, and I can see that his shoulders have slumped forward.

I reach across the table and hold onto his free hand. He looks at our interlaced fingers and then to me. "I'm sorry, it's just hard remembering her that way. She was so weak, and her hair was gone so she wore a lot of head wraps and sometimes wigs. She made sure that us kids never saw her without her head covered, but one night I went downstairs to get a drink and she was in the kitchen washing dishes without her head wrap on. I watched her silently—she didn't notice I was there—so I turned around and went back to my room. I cried all night. It's just, when you're young, your parents are the strongest people you know, so to see her body thinning out and becoming so fragile, it lives in my mind every day. I watched my mom slowly leave this world." I see a single tear roll down his cheek and he quickly swipes it away. I stay silent because I know this is him grieving.

"Anyway, now I'm crying over a plate of lasagna in an Olive Garden. My mom would be laughing at me. She was a huge Olive Garden fan as well. But she passed away in December of 1998. My sisters and I became really close, and we leaned on each other to get through it. I took care of them and pretty much raised them when my dad turned to drinking. Evie and I have stayed close, but Angie moved out when she was eighteen and is attending college in California. We haven't seen her since. She became angry and bitter about my dad and his drinking problem. She felt like he had given up on us, which he had, but I don't think she will ever truly forgive him. She stuck with us until we got him help, but she left shortly after that. Evie is my best friend. And the reason for the pink streaks in our hair"—he plays with his dyed locks as the strands fall over one of his topaz-colored eyes—"it's for my mom. It's like she's with us every day . . . in our own weird way."

"That's truly the sweetest testament, Jeremiah. She sounds like an amazing woman. I wish I could have met her," I say to him with a sympathetic smile.

I start to get a lump in my throat as my emotions creep up on me. It's makes me angry and sad that Claire isn't alive to see her kids as young adults. She doesn't get to be proud of their accomplishments or be here for all their milestones. I wish I could show Claire what an amazing young man she raised her son to become.

It also makes me sad for my mom, the fact that she has so much life to live, and yet she can't see how lucky she is to be able to even breathe and wake up every day. I really am determined to help my mom stop drinking and find happiness again. Life is too short.

✽ ✽ ✽

After we leave the restaurant, we head back to Miah's place. As soon as we enter the door, I see that one of his roommates-slash-bandmates, the singer to be exact, is standing in the kitchen making himself a grilled cheese sandwich. I have yet to meet him, but I don't think Miah realizes because he just nods at him and continues on his way through the kitchen.

"Hey, what's up? My name is Chris. I don't think we've officially met, but I've seen you around and I've heard a lot about you from Jeremiah and Taylor," Chris says, turning away from the stove. He wipes his palms on his jeans and then holds out a hand for mine to accept. I blink, pausing for a second. Sometimes I forget that Taylor's over here more often than I am since she's dating Lars.

"Hey, I'm Cora, but you can call me Cece—whichever, really." I extend my hand and give his a good shake. Miah has stopped in front of the basement door, holding the knob, and is watching my interaction with Chris.

"Oh shit, I'm sorry. I didn't know you two had never met," Miah apologizes, walking back over to me. He places a hand on my low back, slowly touching me up and down my spine. I can tell that he feels bad for not stopping and introducing me. "Chris is the singer of The Restrictions, also my roommate, and also the cleanest and most organized person I know," Miah says, smiling at Chris. Chris returns the gesture and looks back to his grilled cheese on the stove.

"It's really nice to finally meet you, Cece. I've been meaning to ask Miah if you two would be interested in joining my boyfriend, Brett, and me for dinner one night. I think we'd all have a good time." He slides his perfectly golden sandwich off the pan and onto a paper plate and then turns to face us again. Miah looks down at me, waiting for my response.

"Yeah, I would love that," I say, lifting my chin and smiling at Miah.

"Great! I'll plan it out with Miah and then we can go from there." Miah nods at Chris and takes my hand to lead me back to the basement door.

"Nice meeting you, Chris. I can't wait for dinner!" I respond as we start our descent through the door and down the stairs.

"I've been working on something new that I wanted to show you." Miah steps down from the last stair and flicks on the light. Continuing to hold my hand, he leads me over to the same area where he showed me the painting of my eyes. A canvas is sitting on an easel in front of us, and it's a painting of a woman in bright colors of red, orange, yellow, green, purple, and blue. The level of detail is amazing—it looks more like a photograph. When I've taken in the sight of the painting, I turn to Miah next to me. He's still studying his beautiful work of art.

"It's incredible. Do you mind if I ask who it is?"

He stares at his masterpiece for a moment longer, then he faces me and whispers, "It's Claire. That's my mom."

Our hands are still clasped, so I rub my thumb along his knuckles while we both admire his mom through Miah's eyes and memory. "Wow, she was absolutely stunning."

We stand like that for several moments, until Miah's gentle voice cuts through the sadness and silence in the room. "I have never painted her before or had the urge to, but since I met you, I just had to. I meant what I said at the restaurant, you have the same aura as my mom, and I just feel at home with you." He's still looking at the painting, but I'm looking at him.

I think I'm falling in love with this boy.

"Jeremiah, I'm honored, really. I feel the same way when I'm with you. Thank you for letting me be me." Miah turns to me and smiles. He leans in slowly and I rise on my tiptoes to meet him halfway. He softly places his lips on mine and the warmth from him travels through my body again, like the first time we kissed. I part my lips and let him in. Stepping closer to him, I wrap my hands in his hair as our tongues gently twirl and explore each other's mouths. He's holding onto my waist, and as our breathing starts to get heavier, he pulls me in closer and a bit tighter. We continue this way for what feels like ages, breathing heavily and frantically touching each other. He finally breaks away from me and holds me back.

"I'm sorry. I have to stop. I just want more of you, but we really need to go slow, and I want you to lead the way," he says breathlessly. I'm panting as well, but I cup his face in my hands as my heart skips a beat thinking of how considerate Miah is.

"It's okay. I agree, I'm not ready yet . . . I'll let you know when I am. I promise." I give him a soft peck on the lips. I'm relieved he broke away. I've never had sex before and I'm probably not nearly as experienced as he is in that department. Plus, it would be too fast and too soon, and that's not me.

Miah and I make our way upstairs to the living room,

both plopping down on the couch at the same time. After surfing through the channels on TV, we decide to throw on an episode of *Ghost Hunters*. We end up talking for the next hour while it plays in the background. He asks me questions about school and what I want to do after I graduate. I pepper him with questions about performing on stage, what he likes to do for fun, and about his job, which I've never asked him about before. Turns out, he's the customer service manager for a huge insurance company. He admits he enjoys the pay, but he's more interested in making a career for himself and the band. Honestly, I can't blame him.

Eventually I look at my phone and see that it's after eight o'clock. "I'm sorry, Miah, but I should get going. If I'm not home before ten on a school night, my mom will lose it."

"Absolutely. Let's head out," Miah responds.

The drive goes by fast, and when we pull up to my house, I notice that the porch light and my mom's bedroom light are both on, so my mom must be waiting for me to get home. I pause for a moment as I grab the door handle.

"I had a lot of fun today, Little Jetta. Thanks for hanging with me," Miah quickly says before I can open the door.

"Yeah, thank you for helping me forget about my mom for a while. It was nice to get out." I let go of the handle and turn back to him, just as he leans in and looks into my eyes. He's inches from my face. As I take in the familiar smell of him, my stomach starts to tingle. He slowly leans in and kisses me, a soft kiss on the lips that lasts for a minute. I pull away from the kiss as I see out of the corner of my eye that the kitchen light has flicked on.

"Well, I should head in. Call you tomorrow?"

"Can't wait," Miah says with a wink.

I hesitate to get out . . . I want to stay in Miah's car and in the comfort of his touch, scent, and kiss forever. I finally force myself to climb out of the car and walk toward the house, and I can't stop smiling like an idiot as I make my way inside.

CHAPTER EIGHT

Karma's a Bitch . . . or Am I?

December 2005

School has been extremely busy, between end-of-semester projects and exams. My classmates, and myself included, have been buzzing because holiday break is in two weeks. I'm excited by each month that passes because it's another step closer to graduation and freedom. Freedom from this city, my parents, this house . . . but I have a lot to figure out.

I still haven't applied to any colleges and I'm not even sure what I want to do with my life. Community college seems to be my best bet until I figure out what I want to do and become. I picked up a photography class for next semester, so that may be something I enjoy. I've also taken an interest in social media and web design. Who knows where that could lead to as a career? When I think about a future working a nine-to-five job, I don't feel excited. I don't want a "boring" life, but I'm just not sure how *not* to have a boring life.

I know one thing for certain: three months ago, my whole life changed all because of a boy named Jeremiah. I know I shouldn't, but I have been basing a lot of my future decisions on trying to stay close to Miah. We haven't spoken about The Restrictions' summer tour next year, so I don't know what will happen with us. I hope he will still want to be together even when he's on the road with the band.

About three weeks ago, Miah and I officially labeled ourselves as boyfriend and girlfriend, even on MySpace. My heart nearly jumped out of my chest when he put me in his "Top 8" list on MySpace—in spot number one. Things with Miah have been good, more than good, actually. Amazing. We spend our weekends together, going to the movies or out to eat, browsing the record store, and just hanging around his house or mine. The dates I adore the most are when we go to my favorite bookstore downtown. Miah and I both grab a new book and a coffee and then drive back to his place to cuddle up together on his living room couch and read. We don't speak much, but in the silence, I still love his presence. I love to feel him close.

The Restrictions have been performing almost every Saturday. I've been trying to make it to each show, but sometimes I'm not in the mood to hang in a stuffy bar, or the show is limited to ages twenty-one and up. Those are the only weekend nights Miah and I don't get to see each other, but we hang out during the day.

It appears that my mom has started to come around to Miah. I got home from hanging with Taylor one evening and found Miah sitting at the kitchen island next to my mom. He was talking about his mom, Claire, and life with his dad since Claire's passing. Ever since, when Miah comes in the house, my mom acts genuinely happy to see him. Plus, the fact that he's not drinking or doing drugs seems to boost her opinion of him.

I still haven't introduced Miah to my dad . . . I haven't even told my dad anything about him. I've been doing a good job avoiding the topic and dodging any questions my dad has about my "mystery boyfriend." It's not like I see my dad much anyway, probably about twice a month, so it's been easy to keep Miah a secret from him.

I know that talk is coming, though, but I file it away in my brain to worry about later as I drive to school on this dark and cold Monday. Taylor starts basketball after school today, so we've swapped our Monday carpool for Wednesday. I'm a little bummed because I looked forward to my morning drives with Taylor after her wild weekends (much wilder compared to mine). Her stories always added some excitement to the start of the week as she'd recount some random funny thing that happened. There's never a dull moment with Taylor, and that's part of why being her friend is so fun.

I'm heading into the student entrance of the school when Taylor jumps on my back, grabbing my shoulders.

"It's too early to be jumped, Taylor. And, OW!" I'm hunching over in an effort to get her to stop. She does and comes to walk next to me.

"I'm just so excited to see you! I feel like I haven't seen you in years." She's whining and making a pouty face at me.

"Taylor, you saw me Friday night and it's Monday . . . chill." She scrunches her face at me in response.

"Anywayyyy, would you and Miah want to go out to dinner with me and Lars tomorrow night? We are celebrating our two-month anniversary! Lars is going to ask

Chris and Brett if they want to join too." Taylor has always been this way with guys she's dating. She likes to celebrate everything with them and always makes it a point to acknowledge each month they survive putting up with each other. Although, Lars is the most mature and nicest of all the guys Taylor has ever dated, so I'm happy to join them for a celebratory dinner.

"Yeah, let me text Miah and see if he can make it. I'll have to run it by Lucy and get back to you about it tonight."

"Sounds good, Little Jetta." She's smiling and nudges her shoulder into mine. I roll my eyes at her and laugh.

Taylor walks me to chemistry class while telling me all about how Lars plays drums for her when she goes to his house, and how they watch movies with Chris and Brett. I enjoy listening to her talk about Lars and his living situation with the band. It's kind of interesting to hear how the guys live together and interact with each other, without me having to ask Miah. I always wonder how Miah manages to not go insane living with three other men. But when I'm there, it seems like the house is always empty or the guys are in their rooms.

Taylor and I continue walking down the hall as she chats away. We part ways when I approach my classroom. The bell rings, so Taylor hustles four doors down the hall and enters her algebra class.

※ ※ ※

When the final bell rings for the day, I hurry out to my car. As I approach, I notice something stuck beneath the wiper blade on the windshield. I squint my eyes to see if I can make out what it is, but I can't tell.

I really don't need another flyer reminding students to order their senior class rings.

I finally get close enough to realize it's a single tie-dyed rose with a note attached to it. I carefully pull the rose from under the wiper blade. My heartbeat quickens with excitement and a smile spreads across my face. I quickly open the note. Written in perfectly neat, cursive script, it reads:

Just wanted to let you know I was thinking about you. If I did this every time you crossed my mind, your car would be covered in roses. I can't wait to see you again. Hope you had a great day, my Little Jetta. —J

I start giggling to myself. I reread the note two more times before I slip it and the flower into my bag, jump in my car, and send off a text to Miah: *I've never had a surprise like this before in my life. It was so sweet, thank you.*

Then I remember what Taylor asked me and follow up with another message: *Would you want to grab dinner with me, Taylor, Lars, Chris, and Brett tomorrow night?*

I wait five minutes to see if he responds but he doesn't, so I start my car and head home. When I'm driving down my street, I see my mom's car pulling in the driveway just before me. By the time I get into the house, she's already in the kitchen, standing at the sink and rinsing her Tupperware that she used for the day.

"Hey, Ma," I greet her as I plop down on one of the kitchen

island stools, setting my bag on the floor next to me.

"Hey, honey. How was school?" she asks, still busy at the sink.

"It was good. Question: Can I go to dinner tomorrow night with Taylor, Miah, and some guys from Miah's band?"

"Umm, as long as your homework gets done, you're home before nine, and there's no drinking or drugs involved, then it's a yes." She flicks the faucet off and grabs the dish towel from the counter to dry her hands as she walks over to me.

Taking a seat next to me, she has a cautious look on her face. "Cece, I wanted to talk to you about the drinking stuff and things that have been going on between your father and me." She pauses for a moment to gauge my reaction, and I nod my head for her to continue. "A couple of months ago, Jeremiah gave me some names and numbers to call for therapy and help regarding my problem. I've been seeing a therapist nearly every week, and it has helped a lot. I feel really good lately, and I've only been having a glass of wine once a week, and that's enough for me."

I'm shocked, to say the least. The fact that my mom has genuinely taken this seriously and that Miah has had a hand in helping her . . . He's helping me get my mom back, and acknowledging that makes my heart feel like it's about to burst. I jump off my seat and hug my mom tightly.

After we embrace, I sit back down and look at her intently. "Mom, I'm really happy for you. Is there anything I can do to make things easier for you?"

"Yes, there is. I would like us to start doing things together and talking more. I have realized that I want to spend more time with my daughter and not look back and regret that I was selfish while you were going through something painful as well." She grabs my hand and holds it tightly. Her breathing changes to sniffling and tears stain her cheeks. I watch my mom and feel nothing but love and sadness for her. She really is trying, and I admire her for that.

"I would love that. I'm sorry I haven't always been there for you, Mom. I've just felt really lost in the divorce, and I love both you and Dad. I'm pissed at Dad, and I don't know if I'll get over it, but I don't want either of you to think I'm taking sides."

"No, Cora, I would never think you are taking sides. He's your father, and you have every right to see him and do what you need to do. Which brings me to my next topic," she says, wiping her cheeks and taking a deep inhale. "Your father and I spoke, and we would like to sit down with you and go over a plan for your future. Maybe look at some careers you're interested in or colleges you'd like to attend?"

"Wow, you guys spoke, and you want to be in the same room together?" I'm only half-joking.

"Cora, yes . . . We can be mature for the sake of our child," she responds, rolling her eyes.

"Yeah, I would like that. I have some thoughts, so it would be nice to talk to both of you." I agree with my parents. It's time to figure out what I'm going to do with my life since I want to leave this town so badly.

"I'll call your dad and we can set something up. I really love you, Cora." At those last few words, I can feel the tears welling up, but I blink them back for the time being.

"I love you too, Mom." She slides off the stool and heads upstairs. As she ascends and I'm left alone in the kitchen, I let some tears fall. I haven't heard my mom say she loves me and felt like she meant it in a while. I was beginning to think I had lost her or that she resented me for some weird reason for what my dad did. I honestly believe she's on her way to a healthier and happier life, but I still think she needs to get out more. I make a mental note to write up a list of mother-daughter dates that would be fun and exciting for my mom.

Grabbing my bag from the floor, I head up to my room to unpack from the school day. On my way up the stairs, I notice I have a missed call from Miah. I quickly unload the contents of my bag, close my bedroom door behind me, and hit the speed dial button for Miah.

After the second ring, he answers. "Hey! What's up? You okay?"

"Yeah, I'm great. Thank you so much for the rose, it's beautiful," I say, looking over at the single tie-dyed rose sitting on my desk with the note still attached.

"You're welcome. I would love to come to dinner tomorrow night. Chris wanted me to tell you that he's working late tomorrow, so he and Brett won't be able to make it," Miah says.

"Okay, sounds good. I can't wait to see you. I know I just called you, but I should go. I should be working on a thesis I have to write for my chemistry class that's due before holiday break."

"Smart girl. I'll pick you up tomorrow for dinner. Bye, Little Jetta," he responds.

"Bye, Jeremiah...," I want to tell him I love him more than anything, I'm just not sure if he feels the same way yet.

There's a pause before Miah speaks again. Then he replies,

"Bye, Cece."

I flip my phone closed and fall back onto my bed with a heavy sigh.

I hope he loves me too.

* * *

Tonight is our big double-date night with Taylor and Lars at a Mexican restaurant called Loco Cantina. When Miah and I get into the restaurant, the hostess escorts us to a table where Lars and Taylor are already sitting and reading their menus. We say our hellos and then settle in to look at our menus as well. While we wait for the server to come take our order, Taylor and I keep Lars and Miah entertained with our stories about school and all the weird things we both have done since we've been friends.

We order our meals, and as the server leaves with our menus, I decide to finally take in my surroundings and check out the restaurant. "This place is cool. I've never been here before," I say to the table.

Loco Cantina is painted in bright colors of turquoise, orange, red, and yellow, and the walls are covered in stylish murals of the sun and moon. The wooden tabletops have intricate carvings of flowers and cacti.

I want one of these tables.

"They opened a year ago, and they have the *best* burritos in Portland. Hands down," Lars says to me while he dips a chip into salsa.

"Yes, we know. I'm pretty sure I've heard you from across the hall, talking in your sleep about their burritos," Miah teases, smiling at his roommate.

Lars is just about to put another chip in his mouth, but at Miah's comment, he stops and his face drops. "Dude, they're really good. You're going to dream about them too." We all start laughing at him.

I continue my survey of the restaurant until my eyes catch something straight ahead. My breath gets stuck in my throat and my heart crashes to a stop. I swear my blood has frozen in my veins. I can't believe what I'm seeing, so I rub my eyes. It doesn't help. Two tables ahead sits my dad, casually laughing and talking with a younger woman as he occasionally grazes his hand along the top of hers. I keep staring—I can't look away. He seems so relaxed and happy, like they are comfortable with each other. I have the urge to launch over our table and the next and punch him in the face, but I won't. I've started sweating and I'm beginning to have a panic attack as I suck air in and out of my lungs harder and harder to try and catch my breath. I keep reminding myself to stay calm. I don't want to make a scene, and I don't want him to notice me.

Is this his mistress? His paramour? The woman who ruined my family?

"Cece?... Cece? Hello, Cora?!" Miah taps my back, and right before I turn to look at him, I catch my dad's eyes. His mouth drops like he's just been caught in a lie. I can tell he's nervous because he jerks his hand from the woman's. He fumbles and knocks his knife onto the floor. I finally look away from the disaster that's unfolding in front of me.

I try to focus instead on Miah, and his brows are furrowed, genuine concern is painted across his face. "Cora, you look like you just came down with something. Are you okay?" He rubs my forearm, and I suddenly come back into my mind and think of what to say and what to do.

"Ugh, yeah. I'm sorry, I just thought I forgot to turn off my hair straightener." I fake a small laugh and then glance back over to my dad's table. He's still looking, but I quickly avert my eyes as our server brings out our food. Miah accepts my excuse, but I don't think he believes it. He continues to glance at me every so often and he rests his hand on my knee for most of our dinner, like he's tethering me to our table of friends.

Time goes by and I'm picking at my enchiladas, pretending to eat them, when I sense a looming figure beside me, approaching the table.

"Hey, honey. Funny seeing you here." I know that voice, and I was worried this would happen.

Fuck.

I look up to see my dad standing with his hands in his pants pockets and a pained smile on his face. I can tell he's nervous because he's jingling his keys in his pocket—the ultimate sign that Peter Mitchell is uncomfortable.

"Oh hey, Dad." I nervously glance over to Miah and he's staring at me, shocked. I look back at my dad and notice the young woman he was sitting with isn't standing behind him or next to him.

I decide in that moment that I want to see my dad squirm, so I'm going to introduce Miah as my boyfriend. For my final act, I'm going to tell him Miah's age. It makes me furious that he's parading around with his young mistress while my mom has been drinking herself into misery every night. I'm going to hit him where it hurts. I know he won't make a scene in a restaurant, that's not his style. He will act calmly and stew about it until he has a moment to talk to me alone.

I lean into Miah and wrap my arm around his, placing my other hand on his chest. "Dad, this is my boyfriend, Jeremiah. He's twenty-two and lives in a house with his three bandmates, and I hang out there often."

Miah is looking back and forth between my dad and me with a panicked expression on his face. He doesn't say anything and continues glancing between us for several seconds. My dad stares at me with his mouth gaping open. Like a fish out of water, his mouth starts to flap but no words come out. I, on the other hand, am smiling because I'm proud of the agony I've caused within my dad.

Karma's a bitch.

"Hey, Peter!" Taylor shouts from across the table. She's waving at my dad, and I can tell she's definitely trying to ease the tension. My dad looks at her and smirks, but he's not happy to see her. His eyes are filled with fury.

"Oh hey, Taylor, didn't see you over there. How are things going? How are your parents? I haven't seen you in a while."

I don't hesitate to snap back. "Well, if you were around instead of frolicking through town with your mistress, you would see Taylor and your daughter more. But I guess some things are more important than your own child."

"Cora . . . ," Taylor says to me. It comes off as if she's warning me, but she didn't see him sitting with her.

Miah stands up and extends his right hand out to my dad. "Mr. Mitchell, I'm Jeremiah Novak. It's nice to meet you." My dad pauses for a moment and then returns the handshake, begrudgingly.

"Nice to meet you, Jeremiah. I wish I could say I've heard a lot about you, but I honestly haven't heard anything about you." Both my dad and Miah are standing and looking down at me.

"Where did your mystery date go?" I ask my dad.

"Cora, we can talk about that later," he snaps.

"Sure. Maybe later we can also talk about why you decided to wait to approach your daughter until twenty minutes after you noticed her in the restaurant?" I bite right back at him.

"Very nice to meet you, Jeremiah. Taylor, good to see you again. Cora, we will talk later," my dad says as he nods to each one of us. He turns and walks off.

"Bye, Peter!" Taylor says, waving and smiling.

"Very nice to meet you, Mr. Mitchell. I hope to see you again!" Miah shouts, but my dad's almost out the door.

I refuse to watch him leave, so I keep my eyes on my plate. My emotions are at war with each other in my head and in my heart. I want to smoosh my enchiladas in my dad's face, but I also want to cry and storm out of here. Maybe I have anger issues? Or maybe I feel like how any teenager would feel after seeing their dad out with the woman who destroyed their family? I would say the latter.

"Yup. See ya." It's all I can muster up, but it comes out as a whisper when he's already gone.

Miah sits back down and resumes eating his food, but I can feel him glance at me from time to time. I don't look up, for fear of anyone asking me what that was about, because I don't feel like talking about it. The rest of the meal is filled with small talk among the three of them as I continue to spiral and stew in my own thoughts.

Once we've paid the check, we all walk out of the restaurant to say goodbye and head to our cars. Taylor grabs my hand before I jump into Miah's BMW, and I spin to look at her.

"Hey, are you okay?" she asks as her face slumps in sadness.

"Not really. I'll call you later," I answer as I squeeze her hand. She nods and walks to Lars's car as I slide into the passenger seat of Miah's.

When Miah turns on the car, the heat blasts toward us. It's still cold so he clicks on the seat warmers. We remain quiet for most of the ride back to my place. I don't think I have the energy to talk, but I know what I did back there was wrong. At some point, Miah finally breaks the silence.

"Cora, what the hell happened back there? Are things that bad between you and your dad that you always act that way toward him?" His voice is stern. He sounds annoyed, which leads me to break down. I start crying and I can't seem to stop. He takes my hand in his and just lets me get it all out. "We don't have to talk about it, but Cora, I hope you're okay. Who I saw back there is not the Cece I know."

I wipe the tears from my eyes and swipe my coat sleeve under my nose to use as a tissue. "I'm so sorry. I saw him at a table across from us about ten minutes after we sat down. He was sitting with a young woman, who I'm assuming is the one he worked with and left my mom for. He made eye contact with me and didn't even have the fucking balls to come talk to his own daughter until he was leaving—and that girl was already gone." I start to cry harder, to the point where I can't even make a noise if I wanted to.

"Wait, he was in there that whole time and you never said anything to us, and better fucking yet, he didn't acknowledge his daughter?!" Miah's voice is raised, and I can tell he now feels what I'm feeling. "What kind of father does that?" he adds.

"Mine, I guess. I can't describe exactly what I'm feeling, but mostly, I just feel so broken. I finally felt like things in my life were getting better, and he came in and ripped all that happiness away—again. Just like he did when he lost his job because of the affair, and when he told my mom he loved the other woman and wanted a divorce, and again when I watched him pack his stuff and walk out of our house that we shared as a family." Miah pulls to the side of the road and puts his car in park. He fully turns in the driver's seat so he's facing me, but I continue staring out the windshield.

"Listen to me, Cora. Not all men are like that and, unfortunately, dads fuck up. Parents fuck up. I don't want you to go through life thinking this is what marriage and men are like because it's not. I had two parents who loved each other so much. They fought, and they hated each other sometimes, but at the end of the day, they were best friends." He's holding my hand again and stroking my knuckles with his thumb in a comforting motion. I nod at him and wipe my eyes and nose once more.

"I was really scared back there. Your dad looked pissed. I'm pretty sure he was going to kill me, but then I'm pretty sure you would have killed him first." I start laughing and the sadness begins to ease a bit.

"Yeah, I just didn't care at that point. I'm sorry I did that to you," I apologize to him, because in that moment I didn't think of how Miah would feel about me throwing him to the wolves like that, forcing him to fend for himself. It was selfish and immature—I guess this is a lesson for me.

"I accept your apology, I really do. I know that anger got the best of you . . . But Cora, I'm on your team. If there's ever a situation where you are upset or don't know how to handle it, give me a signal and I can help you out." He leans closer and wipes my tears away with his thumb. I nod my head again to signal that I understand. I messed up and should have never done that to Miah *or* Taylor *or* Lars (even though I'm pretty sure Lars missed the whole thing, he was so engulfed in his burrito). I should apologize to them.

Miah reaches for me and wraps his index finger and thumb around my chin, turning my face to his. He softly places his lips on mine for a moment. The warmth and tenderness of his kiss is like a bandage being placed on my self-inflicted wounds, and I begin to feel like myself again.

After I calm down, Miah resumes driving. A song by Social Distortion plays low through the car as we hold hands and remain silent the rest of the way back to my house. Miah drops me off and reassures me that things will get better . . . and I believe him.

I rush to the door and immediately kick off my shoes once I enter the house. I bolt to my room in hopes that I don't run into my mom. Right now, I can't bear to look at her after what happened tonight . . . and I'm not ready to tell her. When I enter my room, I fall onto my bed. I check my phone one last time and decide to explain myself to Taylor tomorrow since I'm too exhausted to talk about anything, especially my feelings. I end up falling asleep fully clothed with my cell phone still in hand.

* * *

I roll out of bed the next morning, throwing on jeans and a sweatshirt. I don't bother to put on makeup or fix my hair, I don't have the motivation. I grab a water bottle from the fridge and head out to pick up Taylor for school. On my way to her house, I grab us two caramel macchiatos from Starbucks to help cheer me up a bit, and as an apology to Taylor. I pull up to the curb in front of her house thirty minutes earlier than usual so we can chat about last night.

Taylor comes out of her house, but she's not wearing her usual smile. She looks tired but not unhappy. When she gets in the car, she eyes the caramel macchiatos sitting in the cup holders and perks up.

"Ohhhhh, for *moi*?" she asks as she places her hand on her chest dramatically.

I shake my head and laugh, "Yes, princess, for you."

She carefully picks up the hot coffee and takes a few sips followed by a long "Mmmmmm" as she holds the cup with both hands and scrunches her face in excitement.

"I was thinking . . . wanna ditch today and either go shop or chill in bed?" she proposes and then takes another long sip of her macchiato. I was thinking the same thing when I forced myself out of bed this morning, honestly, but I pushed through the thought and got ready anyway. By my logic, I'm already a loser since I don't have my future lined up, so the least I can do is still show up for classes. But Taylor's offer is tempting...

"Yes, but let's skip the shopping and just hang around and veg. Mental health day?" I answer.

"Mmm, yes, total mental health day. Last night was traumatic."

I cringe at her words because I know I made it very uncomfortable for everyone involved and even for the innocent bystanders at the restaurant.

I drive back to my house, and we make our way to my room. We both put on sweatpants and plop down on the bed with our macchiatos. Once we're settled, I give Taylor a serious look. "I want to apologize for last night. Before I get into why I acted the way I did, I want to say I'm sorry to you and Lars. I was super immature."

"Cora, I know you like no one else. Let's be honest, it takes a lot for you to get that mean, so I knew something bad had happened. I just couldn't figure out what since you were at the table with us the whole time."

And with that response, I give her the full story. Including Miah's reaction in his car. It's slightly comical that while I'm telling Taylor, she gets just as upset as I did when I saw my dad and his mistress together last night.

"Oh, I totally would have walked my freckled ass to his table and introduced myself to the *thing* he was with. I would have put on a show. Also, don't apologize to me for what happened. It's okay."

I start laughing because although her response wouldn't have been mature either, she totally would have done just that.

She abruptly sits up and looks at me through squinted eyes. "Question: What did she look like?"

I go back in my mind to last night, staring at my dad and the woman at the table, but I don't think I even saw her face. "This is crazy, but all I can remember is long blond hair. I was so focused on my dad, I don't recall anything else about her appearance."

"Next time, remember to get a good look at her so we can judge her."

I laugh and toss a pillow into her lap. "Don't you worry, I will get a super-detailed good look at her next time."

CHAPTER NINE

Emo Girl

It's been about a week since I ran into my dad at Loco Cantina. He hasn't tried calling or stopping by the house since then. I'm not mad about it. I would rather avoid the conversation—or confrontation, I should say, since I usually end up crying when I try to stand my ground with my parents. Which, in turn, means I don't get to air all my grievances, and I end up feeling more frustrated once the conversation is over. So I'm okay with the silence for now.

Christmas is coming up in a week and it will be the first time my family is spending it apart. I'm not entirely sure what my parents' plans are, as far as whom I'm spending Christmas with. I'm sure my mom will tell me what's expected of me at some point. Maybe that's when my dad will speak to me about what happened . . . Yay, merry Christmas to me.

Miah is picking me up tonight to go see a show and then hang at his house after. I'm getting ready in my room when he calls.

"Hey, Cece, bad news. My car won't start so I had to get it towed to the shop. Any way you can come to me?"

I sit for a second as I start to get slightly annoyed that he didn't tell me earlier about his car being towed. "When did you realize your car wouldn't start?" I ask him.

"Oh, this morning when I went to leave for work. I stayed home and waited for the tow truck to come," he answers casually.

Now I'm even more upset. "Sure. Be there in thirty minutes," I say and snap my phone shut without saying goodbye.

I finish getting ready, but I can't figure out why I'm angry with Miah for not telling me sooner that his car wouldn't start. Maybe it's because he waited until ten minutes before he was supposed to be picking me up? It could also be the fact that he stayed home from work and didn't tell me that either. I try to calm myself down and not get so worked up over it. I'll just have to talk to him when I see him.

The entire drive to his place, I go over what I will say to him. When I get to his house, I walk in the front door and close it behind me. I don't see anyone right away, so I continue into the living room. Still no sight of anyone. I look up the stairs, realizing that I've never been to the second floor. Nor have I seen Miah's bedroom before because we always hang out in the living room. I slowly ascend the staircase. I'm still disappointed about the car situation, but now I'm kind of giddy that I get to see Miah's room. I reach the landing and turn left. That's the only way I can go since there's a wall directly in front of me and to the right of me. I walk down the hallway at a leisurely pace, observing the doors to see if I can find Miah's. There are three doors on the left and two on the right. As I continue down the hall, I notice the door to the last room on the right is ajar, and a sliver of light is shining through the crack. I can also hear the low thrums of a bass guitar being played through a speaker, that's how I know for certain it's Miah's room. I lightly knock on the door and the bass stops playing.

"Yo, come in," I hear Miah say.

I open the door to find him sitting on a rolling chair with his bass on his lap. He smiles at me, but I can tell he's a bit hesitant, probably trying to gauge my feelings since I hung up on him.

I look around his room before I make my way over to him. His walls are painted in a terrible light-blue color that does nothing to hide the holes and scuffs all over them, which makes me believe they haven't been painted in a while. He has posters of his favorite bands, pictures of his sisters and mom and a man I assume is his dad since I've never seen him before. Last, I look at his bed. I immediately blush a bit as heat rushes up my body all the way to the tips of my ears. I can't let the thought of him lying in his bed, just in his boxers, hair disheveled and tattoos exposed, consume me right now. I have to talk to him about how mad at him I am...

But man, I would love to wake up to Miah in that bed...

When I finally snap back to reality, I avert my eyes to the picture hanging above his bed. It's a large canvas painting of a beach in vibrant blue and turquoise colors that oddly match Miah's eyes. One look at it and I can tell it's a creation of his. Miah's room is quite clean and organized, but I would expect nothing less of him. He keeps everything organized and clean.

When I finally decide that I've thoroughly looked around

enough, I cross the room to stand near him. He rises from the chair and puts the bass down, leaning it against the amplifier. He turns to me but doesn't move.

"Did I do something to piss you off? You hung up on me and it kind of pissed me off," he says with a stern look on his face. I give myself a moment to answer. Sometimes my words can bite when I'm upset, and I don't want to hurt his feelings by saying something I will regret.

"Yeah, actually, you did. I'm pissed that you waited to tell me your car shit the bed until, like, ten minutes before you were supposed to be at my house. I'm also pissed that you called out of work and didn't tell me. Although, I'm not really sure why I'm pissed about that one . . . but I am."

My anxiety and anger are getting the best of me and I've begun to sweat. Getting things off my chest is hard for me, and I'm nervous about how he will react. But he doesn't react. He doesn't say anything. He stands there, looking down at his hands, picking at them. But what he's picking at? I have no idea. I'm growing impatient now and angrier by the second.

"Are you going to say something or are you just going to make me stand here and stare at you all night?" I snap at him.

Miah looks up from his hands at me and I can tell he's getting frustrated.

"I'm sorry, Cora. I got caught up in the car stuff today and, to be honest, I forgot that we had plans tonight. If you want to know more about why I waited to call you, I can give you that explanation, even though I didn't want you to think I was making excuses."

I nod for him to continue.

"Evie called me saying that she heard from Angie yesterday and . . . Angie's pregnant." If I was unsure of his anger before, I'm sure of it now. I've never heard his tone so harsh. He turns and sits on his bed. Putting his head in his palms, he wipes his hands down his face and lets out a loud sigh.

"I'm sorry, Cora. I just let the news of Angie get the best of me today. I promise if something like this ever happens again, I'll call earlier and keep you in the loop."

Now I feel like a big, stupid jerk. I shouldn't have been so immature about this whole thing . . . I should have just talked to him.

Miah is still sitting on his bed, his elbows on his knees and his chin resting on his fists, so I take a seat next to him. He lifts his head and looks at me when he feels the bed shift next to him under my weight.

"Is your sister Angie okay?" I whisper to him, trying to keep my voice from cracking.

"No, she's not. I don't want you to form an opinion of her without knowing her, but it was a drunken one-night stand, and she doesn't remember who the guy is. That's another reason why I took the day off. Evie and I made calls all day to help her out. Evie is paying to fly her home for Christmas to . . . well, help her with the situation." I'm so mad at myself now and wish I could take it all back. I realize in that moment that it will be the last time I jump to conclusions and get pissed over stupid shit.

I grab his hand and move closer to him so that we are shoulder to shoulder. "I'm sorry, Jeremiah. First, about your sister. And second, you're my first real relationship and I still have a lot of maturing to do. I don't think this will be the last time I let my emotions get the best of me, but I'm going to try to not get upset over stupid things in the future. I'm still so young, and being with you makes me realize that I need to grow up and figure out my own shit. I feel terrible. Please forgive me?"

Miah has tears in his eyes, but he's doing an excellent job of keeping them from falling. "Don't apologize for your feelings. You aren't immature, Cora. I know people who are thirty years old who still act like toddlers." He chuckles and shakes his head before he continues, "I'm aware that this is your first 'real' relationship"—Miah uses his fingers to put air quotes around *real*—"but this is what relationships are. Learning about yourself and the other person, and learning to trust each other. You're letting what people say about our age difference, or your own thoughts about our age difference, get the best of you. You know what I say? Fuck 'em."

He lifts my chin with his thumb and index finger so that my eyes meet his, and he moves closer so that I can feel his breath on my lips. I know I should respond, but I've lost all ability to form thoughts when he's so close.

"Okay," I say breathlessly. I lean into his lips, and as we kiss each other, I know all is forgiven.

Miah moves away slightly and kisses my cheek and then continues kissing me down my neck and behind my ear. My blood is pumping so fast throughout my body that I feel like I may burst into flames. I want to feel him closer. I *need* to feel him closer. With each swipe of his tongue against my neck, my body pulses and I feel it low in my belly and between my thighs.

I've never felt this way before. In fact, before Miah, I never really felt like a woman, as cheesy as it may sound. Miah makes me feel beautiful and sexy just by the way he looks at me, and the way his hands feel on my body and intertwined with mine when we hold hands. He makes me feel like I could wear anything, style my hair however I wanted to, or do my makeup in a crazy way, and he would still think I'm the most beautiful girl in the world.

As I'm trying to wiggle out of my jacket, he helps ease it off and tosses it on the rolling chair he was sitting on not too long ago. He leans back and is looking at me with passion. I can still see a hint of sadness in his eyes. We are both breathing heavily when he asks, "Is this okay?"

I immediately nod my head and whisper, "Yes." I don't need time to think about it.

We crash back into each other. Our lips connect and our tongues are moving frantically. My hands are in his hair, gripping hard onto the black-and-pink strands as if I'm going to fly away with how out of my body I feel right now. His hands are up my shirt, feeling my back and cupping my breasts over my bra. I break away to catch my breath and he looks at me concerned, as if he went too far.

"Just catching my breath," I reassure him.

Miah stands up and moves toward the door, gently closing it. He turns on a lamp sitting on a nightstand between the bed and the door, and he flicks a switch on the wall, turning off the light overhead. I watch him open the drawer to the nightstand and take out a condom before he walks back over to me. I wrap my arms around my chest as I wait for him to return to the bed. My body feels cold and lost without him, and I long for his warmth again.

"You're in control, okay?" he whispers to me as he sits back down on the mattress. I give a simple nod, because I know Jeremiah cares for me and would never push me to do something I wasn't comfortable doing.

Feeling confident, I stand up in front of Miah and slowly pull my shirt up over my head, exposing my hot-pink bra. I bend and slide my jeans off next, revealing matching hot-pink panties. When I stand up straight again, I notice Miah has a playful smirk on his face. I falter a bit in my confidence and bite my bottom lip.

Oh crap, he doesn't like something he sees. I knew I should have run more this fall.

"I would have never guessed your bra would be that color," Miah says, laughing.

"What does that mean?" I retort, smiling and placing my hands on my hips. My confidence comes back when I realize he is surprised by my color choice. I guess I shouldn't have been so hard on myself about my body.

Remember to work on jumping to conclusions, Cora . . .

"You're stunning, Cora," Miah says almost reverently. His eyes soften as he looks up at me. Miah tugs his shirt off over his head and tosses it behind me onto the floor. I move closer and kneel on the floor before him, between his legs. I unzip his pants for him and notice he's begun to get hard already. He watches me with hooded eyes, and it makes me warm between my thighs again.

His chest is toned, with hair on his pecs. Situated perfectly on his stomach is a large, intricate tattoo of an old colonial ship piercing through high waves. I run my fingers along the outline of the ship, taking in the way the tattoo looks on his body. Miah is looking down at me still, watching me trace his tattoo while strands of his hair fall onto his forehead and over his topaz eyes.

"It's amazing," I say as I stop moving my fingers and meet his gaze. The way he's looking at me, like he's taking in the sight of me, makes me feel wanted and beautiful—and I've never felt either of those things in my life. I've never been told I was beautiful before. I mean sure, maybe by my parents when I dressed up for dances or parties, but never by a guy, and especially not with my body so exposed.

"Yeah?" he asks.

Miah pulls me up to stand and gently pushes me back to lie on the bed. Switching spots with me, he bends to remove his pants and then his boxers.

I look him up and down hungrily.

I can't believe all that is all mine.

Miah's body is well taken care of, and it shows. My hands are begging to feel the rest of him. Climbing onto the bed again, he bends his head to my leg and starts kissing his way up my calf, all the way to my thigh until his nose is grazing me in between my thighs. I can feel the heat from his breath seeping through my panties, sending chills all over my body. Suddenly, I feel his mouth on me, his teeth are nibbling on my nub through the fabric. It sends waves of pleasure up to my stomach and all the way to my breasts and heart.

Miah reaches a hand up and works it under my bra so that he is caressing my bare breast. His mouth continues below while his thumb works in circles over my hard nipple. I arch my back, wanting to feel more of his mouth—I want him to just rip off my panties already. He must hear my thoughts because he stops and lifts my bum for me. He pulls my panties down and off completely.

Miah sits back on his heels, pausing a moment while I lay on his bed in my hot-pink bra. He looks down at my body, almost like he's hesitant to go further . . . but then he bends his head between my legs again. He begins to lick his way up my stomach and chest. He reaches a hand behind my back and unclasps my bra, and I toss it aside, exposing my breasts. Miah cups my breasts in his hands and alternates between them, sucking and licking my nipples. It makes me even wetter and I want to push his head back down between my thighs, but I fight the urge.

He suddenly stops and moves so we are eye to eye. Miah's gaze is piercing, like he's searching for something he lost.

"I love you, Cora," he whispers, out of breath.

I place my hands on either side of his face, admiring how perfect Jeremiah is to me.

"I love you too, Jeremiah," I respond, lifting myself onto my elbows to kiss him.

We spend the rest of the night exploring each other's bodies, holding each other close, and moving together in a perfect rhythm. Even with him inside me, I still want to feel him closer. It is passionate and thrilling and hot and sweaty and nothing like I have ever experienced before. It's the kind of love I've seen in movies and read about in books, but I always thought it never happened like that. Those scenes weren't what love was like in real life. But I was wrong, because this feels just like a movie. It is perfect.

* * *

We never make it to that show we were supposed to see. Late that night, I'm resting on Jeremiah's chest with his arm slung around me. His thumb rubs up and down my hip bone, creating goosebumps across my body by the softness of this touch. I'm tracing his tattoo again, pretending to color in the details with an imaginary crayon.

"Why did you laugh at my bra?" I say, breaking the silence. His chest and stomach start moving beneath my head as he stifles more laughter.

"I didn't expect you to be a hot-pink-bra kinda girl, more like a gray- or black-bra-and-panties kinda girl."

I playfully slap his chest. "That's not very nice. You make it seem like I'm some emo girl who coordinates her emotions to her panties. I can be super girly, you know? I've got pink and purple stuff."

"Oh . . . you have purple stuff too? Will I get to see the purple stuff on my floor too, or . . . ?" he says in a low, sultry voice.

My body responds again, but I push away the thought of us tangled together as I prop myself up to look at him. I rest my chin on the top of my hand that's on his chest. He's looking down at me, and I can tell in this moment he's relaxed and has forgotten about earlier today. Miah starts playing with my hair, continuously putting strands behind my ears.

"Can I ask you a serious question?" It's something I have

thought about but haven't had the nerve to talk to him about until now.

"Of course. You can ask me anything, you know that."

"If we are still together when summer comes, after I graduate . . . how are we going to make this work when you're on tour?" I'm scared he will be so busy playing shows and having fun that he will forget about me while he's away. I'm afraid he will meet someone else . . . someone his own age.

"What do you mean by 'how'? I'll call you every day, and we have breaks on the tour so I will fly home to see you." He grips my hip reassuringly, but my doubts still sit with me.

"I know, but I'm scared, Miah. It makes me sick to my stomach. I don't want to lose you." At that, Miah lifts us up and turns me so we are sitting and facing each other on his bed. He holds my hands in his as he looks into my eyes.

"Do you trust me, Cora?" Miah asks.

"Yes, absolutely," I respond without needing to think about the question.

"Then you need to trust that we will make it. I'm not looking for anyone else. I'm going to be busy on the road, but there won't be a second when I don't think about you. I love you and I mean it, Cora. What you're feeling is what I'm feeling too—don't doubt that." He leans in and kisses me hard. Tears roll down my cheeks and onto our lips. I am scared. I'm going to miss him so much.

CHAPTER TEN

Emo Boy

Jeremiah

It irritates me that Cora hung up on me, but I can't worry about that right now when all I can think about is Angie. I want to be mad at Angie for being so reckless, but how can I be? She's a junior in college, living her life and having fun. I still want to find the guy and punch him in the face for sleeping with a girl who was too drunk to function. It takes two to tango, though. How do you have sex with someone and not even know their name? Another question I will never ask, nor do I ever care to learn the answer from experience. I'm just glad I have Evie to help navigate this. I'm no good with this stuff—and I have no idea what Angie could possibly be going through. She must be pretty scared if she called me for help. She hasn't called me in years. Not even to say hi.

I pick up my bass and sit down in my desk chair. I flip the switch on the small amp that's sitting on the floor next to me. This is my attempt at blowing off some steam before Cora arrives. I'm pissed that she's pissed at me for no reason, and I need to calm my mind so that I don't say something stupid.

Mindlessly, I practice our songs while I think about Cora. God, I love her. I haven't told her yet, but she's all I think about all day . . . she just always pops into my head. I know people think it's weird for me to be dating a teenager, but she doesn't act like a teenager. She's smart, and she's unlike any other seventeen-year-old I've ever met. The past couple of years have been tough for her, and I think her parents put her in a position where she needed to grow up pretty quickly. I feel like she's lived most of her life for other people, always carrying their problems on her back. I want her to live for herself and have fun, and I want to be next to her while she does it so I can watch that damn beautiful smile stretch across her face. The one where her cheeks plump up under her eyes because she's smiling so hard and you know she's genuinely happy, without a care in the world . . . As I said, I know what people think about us, but I love her and she knows I respect her. That's all that matters.

I hear a light tap on my door and respond, "Yo, come in." I know it's Cora because the rest of the guys are all out tonight and I'm the only one home.

Our eyes meet and I give her a little smile, but she doesn't return the gesture. She doesn't come over to me right away. Instead, she starts looking at my walls and meandering around my room. I go back to plucking the strings of my bass, watching Cora from under my lashes and admiring her from afar. She has a small scowl on her face, her lips are slightly turned down, so I know she's still upset. I'm calm and ready for whatever she has to say. I know I'll have to tell her about Angie, but whatever I did to make Cora angry, I don't want her to think I'm using Angie's situation as a get-out-of-jail-free card.

When I lift my head to look at Cora again, I see her eyeing the canvas hanging above my bed. She studies it for a full minute. I know she can tell it's one of my paintings. When she finally starts to come toward me, I quickly jump out of my chair so that she doesn't think I was a creep for watching her. I put my bass down and turn back toward her. It looks as though her scowl has deepened, so I stand still even though I want to reach out to her and hold her tightly in my arms so we can skip this fight and just be happy again.

"Did I do something to piss you off? You hung up on me and it kind of pissed me off," I say to break the silence. Instead of dancing around the issue, I'm going to cut right to it. Cora hesitates to answer, and her brows form a V shape in the middle of her forehead, as if she's concentrating on how to verbalize her anger.

"Yeah, actually, you did. I'm pissed that you waited to tell me your car shit the bed until, like, ten minutes before you were supposed to be at my house. I'm also pissed that you called out of work and didn't tell me. Although, I'm not really sure why I'm pissed about that one . . . but I am," Cora shoots off with her voice slightly raised. I can tell by the way sweat is glistening off her forehead that she's not good at getting things off her chest. Another thing her parents probably neglected to help her with while they were busy cheating and arguing.

I look down at my hands and absentmindedly begin to scratch at my palms while I get lost in my thoughts. I should tell her about my sister, but again, I don't want use Angie's situation as my excuse.

"Are you going to say something or are you just going to make me stand here and stare at you all night?" Cora snaps at me. Her voice has jumped another octave, so I know I should finally give her an answer.

"I'm sorry, Cora. I got caught up in the car stuff today and, to be honest, I forgot that we had plans tonight. If you want to know more about why I waited to call you, I can give you that explanation, even though I didn't want you to think I was making excuses."

I lied. I didn't forget we had plans. I'm just biding my time before I tell her the real reason I'm a mess today. I couldn't possibly sit at work all day with the news of Angie on my mind. The car stuff doesn't bother me, it's all a part of life. Sometimes the materialistic shit breaks, but it's not a bad life, just a bad day. But for me, it's been a pretty fucking terrible day. Not because my sister is pregnant, but because of the fact that Angie's out in California, alone, and I can't be there for her the way I want to be. This is my fault. I should have called her more, flew out to see her, paid for her to fly back home more often . . . but it's too late. I hold back the tears. I don't want Cora to see me cry. Not yet.

She nods for me to continue.

"Evie called me saying that she heard from Angie yesterday and . . . Angie's pregnant." Cora's face falters a bit as her expression turns less angry and more sympathetic. This is what I didn't want to happen. I'm mentally exhausted from today, so I turn and plop down on my bed. I wipe my hands down my face in an attempt to rub my eyes free from the tears that never fell.

"I'm sorry, Cora. I just let the news of Angie get the best

of me today. I promise if something like this ever happens again, I'll call earlier and keep you in the loop."

Cora is standing in front of me while I sit on the bed. She keeps clenching and unclenching her fists. I can't bear to look at her when she's on the verge of tears, especially if I'm the cause. I can see why she's upset, I truly can. I should have texted or called her earlier in the day to let her know about my car. I should have thought about her feelings. I was wrong to leave her in the dark for so long.

With my elbows on my knees and my chin resting on my fists, I take deep breaths to release my feelings of frustration, anger, and sadness before Cora and I continue our conversation. I don't want to hurt her. I want to tell her I love her. Hindsight's twenty-twenty, and I know now I should have said I was sorry when I saw her foot cross the threshold to my room.

I hear Cora release a small sigh. It's a strong indication that she's just as defeated as I am, and her anger has subsided. Feeling the mattress dip as she takes a seat next to me, I look her in the eyes. I always find comfort in her eyes.

"Is your sister Angie okay?" Cora whispers. Her voice cracks slightly, like a record on a turntable when it's worn and bent from use and improper handling. I need to remember that Cora is already dealing with so much in her life and I can't snap at her over my own insecurities.

I'm going to be a better boyfriend. I'm not a selfish high school kid like she's used to.

"No, she's not. I don't want you to form an opinion of her without knowing her, but it was a drunken one-night stand, and she doesn't remember who the guy is. That's another reason why I took the day off. Evie and I made calls all day to help her out. Evie is paying to fly her home for Christmas to . . . well, help her with the situation."

Cora grabs my hand and scooches closer so we are shoulder to shoulder. "I'm sorry, Jeremiah. First, about your sister. And second, you're my first real relationship and I still have a lot of maturing to do. I don't think this will be the last time I let my emotions get the best of me, but I'm going to try to not get upset over stupid things in the future. I'm still so young, and being with you makes me realize that I need to grow up and figure out my own shit. I feel terrible. Please forgive me?"

My eyes well up again, and small pools of tears rest on my bottom lids, threatening to spill over. I swallow hard with the effort to keep them from falling.

God, when did I become so emotional?

"Don't apologize for your feelings. You aren't immature, Cora. I know people who are thirty years old who still act like toddlers." I chuckle and shake my head before continuing, "I'm aware that this is your first 'real' relationship"—I use air quotes around *real*, as she called it—"but this is what relationships are. Learning about yourself and the other person, and learning to trust each other. You're letting what people say about our age difference, or your own thoughts about our age difference, get the best of you. You know what I say? Fuck 'em."

Cora bows her head down, as if she's ashamed. I gently tilt her chin so that our eyes meet, and I move closer. It takes all my willpower to fight the urge to hold her and kiss her, but I wait to see if she's ready to let this all blow over.

"Okay," she says breathlessly and leans her lips into mine.

We gently kiss each other for a few moments. I want more of Cora, but I don't want to make her feel pressured into anything. I decide to stick to kissing until she's ready for more. I don't even care when that will be, as long as she's still mine.

Wanting to feel more of her skin with my lips, I kiss Cora's cheek and down her neck. When she dips her head back, I continue to kiss her behind her ear. With my lips on her pulse, I can feel that her heart is beating fast. Cora releases a small moan each time my tongue swipes across the sensitive skin on her neck and on her ear. It turns me on that I'm making her feel good, so I continue. All I can smell is the floral scent of her shampoo, and all I can taste is the saltiness and sweetness of her skin.

She's so fucking beautiful, inside and out. I'm so lucky.

Stopping momentarily, I help Cora out of her jacket. I can feel her body getting warm against me and I want her to be comfortable. Once her jacket is off, I toss it aside, and it lands on my desk chair. I turn back to Cora, looking for validation in her big brown eyes with the green flecks I love so much. If this is what she wants . . . I'm out of breath from how turned on I am and the work it took to get her jacket off, but I want more. I need to know if she does too.

"Is this okay?" I ask.

Without hesitation, Cora nods her head and whispers, "Yes."

Our mouths come together again and we hit each other hard. My lips hurt for a moment but it doesn't bother me one bit. Cora grips the back of my head, pulling strands of my hair into her fingers as if to bring me closer, but I'm as close as I'll ever be.

I don't plan on leaving her anytime soon.

I move my hands under her shirt, feeling her bare back and then cupping her breasts over her bra. She places her hands on my chest and gently pushes me away. I cock an eyebrow at her wondering if I went too far, but she smiles and says, "Just catching my breath."

I stand and make my way to the bedroom door. I close it and lean over to switch on a table lamp on my nightstand. I flick the switch on the wall to turn off the overhead light, and before I head back to Cora, I open the nightstand drawer and pull out a condom.

As I resume my position next to Cora on the bed, I whisper, "You're in control, okay?" I need her to know I mean it, so I look at her intently.

Cora responds by nodding once. She stands up in front of me and slowly pulls her shirt up over her head. My eyes are drawn to her hot-pink bra, and I'm so surprised that I smirk. Cora slides her pants off next, revealing her hot-pink panties to me. Did I mention how fucking beautiful she is? I can't stop taking in the curves of her body. Cora's breasts sit perky and full in her bra. Her brightly colored underwear is slightly see-through, showing just a hint of her lips. I can see her panties are already wet. My cock hardens with every beat of my heart.

I can tell she's self-conscious when she hunches over a bit and begins biting her bottom lip.

"I would have never guessed your bra would be that color," I say, laughing.

"What does that mean?" Cora smiles widely at me and places her hands on her exposed hips. I can't provide her with an answer at the moment when she looks so gorgeous standing there.

"You're stunning, Cora," I softly say, looking up at her.

I lift my shirt up and over my head, tossing it on the floor. Cora comes closer and kneels down in front of me to unzip my pants. I watch her as she concentrates on the task at hand. I can feel my cock continue to strengthen.

When Cora finishes unzipping my pants, her eyes move over my chest as if she's amazed by what she's found. She lightly runs her fingers along the outline of my stomach tattoo, sending chills through my whole body. Her touch feels electric, so I just sit back and watch.

She stops and looks up at me with a heated look in her eyes, "It's amazing."

"Yeah?" I respond. It's a rhetorical question... I don't care for an answer right now.

I pull Cora up from her kneeling position and stand so I can switch spots with her. She doesn't resist me as I guide her to lie on the bed. I bend over and remove my pants and then my boxers. Cora is leaning back on the bed, resting on her elbows. Her eyes narrow in on my cock as she gently licks her lips. I crawl toward her legs and slowly kiss my way up her calf and down into her thigh until my nose is grazing the wet spot on her panties. She shivers and I notice she has goosebumps on her thighs. I'm so turned on that I need to taste her, I can't wait a moment longer. I slowly work my tongue over her panties, licking and sucking her clit. Cora arches her back and moans, so I suck a bit harder.

I reach my hand up her stomach and under her bra so I can hold her breast. I simultaneously work my thumb in slow circles over her hard nipple, as my tongue works circles on her panties just above her clit. I want to feel Cora's bare skin on mine and taste her, I need more of her. I lift her ass and work her panties out from underneath her and down her legs, discarding them on the floor.

I kneel on the bed in front of her, waiting to see if Cora wants this, if she wants to take this all the way . . . but she doesn't stop me. I bend down in between her thighs again to taste the now-bare skin that's exposed to me. Her legs twitch with every swirl of my tongue, which sets me on fire wanting more. Gently kissing my way up her stomach, I take in each freckle. Her freckles are like a constellation of stars leading me to her still-covered breasts. At this moment, I can't stand this damn pink bra, so I reach behind Cora's back and unclasp it. She slips the straps from her shoulders, tossing her bra on the bed. Seeing her completely naked in my bed, looking like an angel, sends me into overdrive. I take both of her breasts in my hands and work my way between them, licking and gently sucking, make sure to give them both the attention they need.

I suddenly stop and lift my head to look her in the eyes.

"I love you, Cora," I whisper.

Cora places her hands on my cheeks with a loving smile on her face. Softly she says, "I love you too, Jeremiah." She carefully lifts herself onto her elbows and gently kisses my lips.

She needs to know that I truly love her. Someone on this earth thinks she's an amazing woman. That she deserves the world and more.

The next few hours of my life were an experience I'll never forget. I guided her as she took control of what she wanted, turning into a fucking warrior goddess. It was a beautiful mess.

I never want to let go of this girl. I think I want her for life ... if she'll have me.

CHAPTER ELEVEN

Holly Jolly Christmas

It's Christmas Eve and I'm spending the day with my dad. He called my mom, and they ironed out the "agenda" for the holidays. I will be celebrating Christmas Eve with my dad, and then Christmas morning will be with my mom. Miah invited me over to his dad's for Christmas dinner with his family, so I'll be spending the night with the Novaks and meeting his dad and Angie for the first time. My mom agreed to let me stay the night with Miah, as long as I "behave." At first, I felt guilty for leaving my mom alone on Christmas, but when I asked her, she let me know that Aunt Karen (my mom's sister) and my cousins are coming to share dinner with her and would be staying at the house. I'm glad she told me or I wouldn't have said yes to Miah's invitation.

It's three o'clock and I've started the drive to my dad's condominium in Biddeford. I haven't spoken to him since the Loco Cantina debacle. Instead of trying to address it over text messages, I've decided that I would rather talk about what happened face to face. I will listen to what he has to say, even if I always will (slightly) resent him for the rest of my life, no matter what his excuse or reasoning is.

I brake and turn down the Christmas music that's blaring through the car when my Garmin indicates that the destination is ahead on my left. I pull up to his condo, which is bedecked in bright, multicolored Christmas lights that glow under a thin layer of snow. I can tell he's put some effort into decorating his place. My dad knows that I love Christmas, particularly for the decorations . . . and he also knows that I love to give gifts. It makes me feel good inside to watch someone open the perfect present and be surprised. My dad used to laugh and tell me that I was a "different" child, since most kids wanted to open gifts, not give them.

When I approach the door, I hesitate on whether to knock or just enter. I guess this is how it goes when you don't know your parents anymore and they no longer feel like home. Before I can make up my mind, the door swings open and my dad is standing on the other side smiling, wearing a bright-red Santa hat.

"Hey, honey! Welcome, come in!" He takes the three perfectly wrapped gifts out of my arms and stands next to the door while I enter. I take off my boots and coat, and my dad hangs my coat on a hook next to the door. He guides me into the kitchen, and when I reach the middle of the room, I spin around to get a good look at his place. It's a decent-sized condo and everything looks new and clean.

My dad notices. "Let me give you a tour. How was the drive?"

I follow him as he leads me out of the kitchen and into the living room. "Not bad. Surprisingly quick and easy."

"Good, good. I've been getting the place ready for your visit. I know how much you love Christmas decorations, so I hope they didn't disappoint."

The living room is nice and cozy. My dad has a fire going with *National Lampoon's Christmas Vacation* playing on the TV. There's a small, but real, Christmas tree in the corner of the room complete with some wrapped presents and a red-and-white tree skirt underneath. He heads over to the tree, still holding the gifts I brought, and places them on the tree skirt to join the others.

"This is nice, Dad. Great job on the tree. It's perfect." My dad smiles at my response and nods.

"C'mon, kiddo, let's continue the tour." He waves his hand for me to keep following him, so I do. The condo is one level, making it a quick tour. There are two bedrooms, and he saves "mine" for last. When he enters the room, he extends his arms out like he's Vanna White on *Wheel of Fortune*, clearly excited for me to see "my room."

The walls of the room are painted light purple, but nothing is hung on them. There's a queen-size bed in the middle of the room, with a purple comforter set to match the walls. A large stereo system sits on top of a dresser, and a CD tower stands next to the dresser with one CD in it. I walk into the room and slowly look around. I can't resist picking up the CD, noticing it's *NSYNC's debut album from when I was about ten.

*Nice try, Dad. But I outgrew *NSYNC about five years ago . . .*

I slide it back into the rack and turn to face my dad. "The room is great, Dad. Really, I appreciate you making a space for me here." My dad steps closer to me and places his hands on his hips while he spins in a circle to take a good look at the room.

"It's not much, but it's a start. I can get you extra clothes, CDs . . . whatever you need so that you have stuff here as well as at your mom's."

I start to feel guilty when he mentions my mom. I don't think I can leave her alone in that house by herself. Especially not to visit my dad's "new" home. Plus, that house will always be my home.

. . . Right?

I swallow the lump in my throat and push the sadness away to fake some happiness.

"Thanks, Dad," I say with a faint smile.

We walk back to the living room, and I sit down on the couch in front of the fireplace as my dad heads to the kitchen. He spends the next fifteen minutes getting the table set for dinner and pulling baked ziti out of the oven. There's no need for me to even look in the kitchen to know what he's cooking. Baked ziti is our Christmas Eve tradition.

"All right, Cora, dinner is ready. What can I get you to drink?" My dad calls from the kitchen.

"A water is good, thanks," I respond as I slowly get off the couch.

He brings two glasses of water and we sit down at the kitchen island. We eat in silence for a bit because we both know what's coming. I can't take how quiet it's become, so I decide to just lay it all out in the open.

"Was that girl at the restaurant the one you cheated on Mom with?" I blurt out, looking down at my plate. My dad picks up his water and takes a few gulps before placing it back down.

"Yes. Her name is Anne." He's so quiet that it comes out

almost as a whisper. He takes the Santa hat off and places it on the island, then he dabs a napkin on his forehead to rid himself of the sweat above his brow.

"Cora, I'm sorry about what happened at that restaurant. I didn't know what to do when I saw you. I could try to explain what was going on in my mind, but you would never believe me."

"I won't ever understand why you cheated. Why not just get a divorce? Could you not keep it in your pants that long? You had to just go for it and hurt Mom and me?!" I've started to shout as I look him dead in the eyes.

"Cora, don't talk to me that way," my dad shouts back. With his response, I begin to deflate. I may not be little anymore, but I still feel intimidated when he yells at me. "Yes, I cheated on your mom with Anne. I didn't mean for it to happen. Look, your mom and I were having marital problems before I lost my job and before I cheated. Things weren't as perfect as we portrayed them to be for a long time. We promised each other that we would keep the peace so that you could have a happy childhood."

"So you just couldn't keep your façade going until after the divorce was finalized? You just *had* to let it all unravel at the most important time of my fucking life? When I'm supposed to be making memories, having fun, and getting ready to become an adult?"

"It's a little more difficult than that, Cora. I don't want to get into the details of mine and your mom's marriage right now, especially without her here to talk about it as well. I'm sorry for what happened at the restaurant. I love you so much, and I want us to get through this and to build back our relationship." He reaches over and takes my hand in his. I fight the urge to jerk my hand away.

I want to forgive him, but I don't want to betray my mom. I want the old relationship I had with my dad back, but I don't think it will ever be the same as what we once had.

"Relationships are hard. Someday you'll understand when you are married and have kids of your own. I didn't do the right thing. I'm not asking you to forgive me, but I don't want to lose you, Cece."

I bite my bottom lip as I contemplate my next words and what I should do. Silent tears start to trickle down my face and I quickly wipe them away. "Yeah. I can try." It's all I can say right now. After a moment, he squeezes my hand before he goes back to eating.

"So, tell me about Jeremiah," he says in a curious tone, which implies that he's unsure about how to tackle this subject.

I can't help but giggle as I take a bite of my ziti. After I chew and swallow, loving the anticipation that's building and keeping him on his toes, I respond, "He's amazing and I would really like for you to get to know him."

"Yeah, well, I'm going to meet him if you want to continue to see this boy. Your mom told me a little bit about him, but I would like to find out what he's about for myself." He's looking over at me, brows pinched together. He looks like any concerned father would.

"Dad, seriously, he's a good guy. You can trust me, and him."

"Well, I'll believe it when I know more about him." I sigh and shake my head back and forth.

"Listen, I could say the same about Anne . . . Don't be so quick to judge." Now it's my dad's turn to shake his head.

We finish our ziti and move to the living room to open gifts. I got my dad a bottle of his favorite cologne and a framed picture of us posing in front of my Jetta. It was the day we brought the car home, and we were both so excited. We have matching large, proud smiles on our faces. It's a gift for his new place, so he has a picture of us together to hang on his wall. After he opens it, he keeps picking up the frame and gazing at the photo, as if he longs to relive that day.

I do too.

I think about that day a lot. I wish I could reverse time and go back to being that happy with him again. But I didn't have Miah then, so I suppose I'd rather not go back in time.

My dad watches as I open my gifts now. The first is a box filled with a few gadgets for my car, including a rearview mirror charm with a flower on it, some cleaning supplies, a car waste basket, and other things only he would think of. The second gift I open is a brand-new iPod. I sit with the box in my hands, unsure of what to say. I'm shocked because most of the kids in my school who own an iPod are ones whose parents have never lost their job. It's way too much, but it's such an awesome gift . . . I could get rid of my crummy old Walkman and just carry around this tiny little rectangle. I want to thank him but kindly decline the gift, knowing I can't accept it. I look up and see that he's so excited and eagerly waiting for my reaction.

"So . . . do you love it or what?" he asks as he walks toward the couch and sits next to me. "It's called an iPod. You put all your music on it and then pop some headphones into the jack and *bam*! You can listen to your music anywhere! The guy at Radio Shack said these are all the rage with teens these days." I can't help but laugh at how much of a dad he sounds like right now.

"Dad, I can't take this. These are so much money. I appreciate the thought, but it's too much." I start to hand the box back to him when he holds his hand up and gently shoves it back onto my lap.

"Cece, I can afford it. I've got a great job and money saved up. We are okay. Don't you worry about money. Take the iPod and enjoy it! Now, let's open it up and get it going before you head out. I bought you a cord to listen to it in your car too." I sit silently, just staring at him while he smiles brightly back at me. I feel the guilt creep in as my mom pops into my head.

Will she be upset with me that I accepted such an expensive gift from him? Will she be upset that he got me such an expensive gift?

I finally clear my thoughts of guilt and decide that I'm going to take the damn iPod. I deserve this.

"Let's get it going," I say, smiling back at my dad.

We spend the rest of the evening getting my new iPod up and running. He helps me set up an iTunes account and upload some music onto it for the ride back to Portland. It's starting to get late, so I decide to head home. My dad is sad that I'm not staying with him for the night, but he understands I only have the morning to spend with my mom before I go to Miah's for dinner.

When I get in my car, it's already running and the windows are scraped clean of ice. Apparently my dad went out to warm up my car and get it ready for me while I packed up my presents and prepared to leave. When I first got my Jetta for my birthday last March, he used to get up before me and clean the snow and ice off my car so that I didn't have to wake up any earlier to do it. During my drive home tonight, I think about all the small things my dad used to do for my mom and me when he lived at home. He was always a good dad, and I guess that's why this sucks so much.

* * *

I wake up the next morning to the smell of coffee and bacon wafting through my bedroom. I jump up, grab my cell phone from my nightstand, and head downstairs to the kitchen. My mom is standing at the stove flipping pancakes when I sit down on a stool at the island.

"Merry Christmas, Mom." My mom jumps, not knowing I entered the kitchen.

She gasps and turns to me. "Oh dear god, Cora, you almost killed me on Christmas!" She starts laughing and turns back to the stove. "Merry Christmas, Cora. How was your dad's?" I debate whether I should tell her he got me an iPod or if I should just leave it alone. I decide to let her know since she will probably see me with it at some point.

"It was all right. His condo is nice and he had some Christmas decorations up, so that was cool."

She sets a plate in front of me with a stack of pancakes and some bacon. "That's nice. Did he get you anything good?" She comes around the island and takes a seat next to me with her own plate of eggs, bacon, and toast. It's sweet that even though she hates the smell of syrup, she loves me enough to put up with it.

"Um, yeah. Please don't be mad, but he bought me an iPod." I rush out the words.

"Oh yeah, he told me he was thinking about getting you one. I would never be mad about that, Cora." She butters her toast and takes a bite. "After this, would you want to turn on some Christmas music and open gifts? I know Jeremiah's going to be here at three, so we should get our day going."

"Yeah, works for me," I respond. Relaxing into my chair, I release the tension in my shoulders I didn't even know was there until I heard my mom's reaction to the iPod. I'm proud of my dad for being considerate and letting her know that he would be getting me one for Christmas. My mom doesn't make a ton of money working at the school, and I didn't want her to feel ashamed if she couldn't afford a gift as costly as that.

We finish breakfast and head to the family room where the Christmas tree is situated in the middle of the large bay window. The tree has been in the same spot every year since I can remember. My mom is a traditionalist when it comes to Christmas. It was my grandma's favorite holiday, so my mom tries to keep the family traditions going. A lot of the decorations around the house were my grandma's, and it provides a very retro vibe, which I love. Same with the ornaments on the tree, but my mom still has the ones that I created while in elementary school placed sporadically on the branches.

My mom and I sit next to each other on the couch, taking turns opening our gifts while Christmas music blasts throughout the house. Every Christmas, my mom always gets me the essentials, which is nice because I'm usually in need of new underwear and socks by the time December rolls around. She also got me a few pairs of jeans from American Eagle and some of my favorite bands' T-shirts to go with the jeans. I decided to get my mom a gift card to Starbucks and a pass to a local yoga studio for four classes. She kept telling me she would love to try yoga, so I figured I would help her get started.

"Cora! This is such a great idea. I love it!" My mom is so excited about the classes that she hugs me tightly to show her appreciation. "Come with me—it will be fun. It would help you with anxiety and me with my depression."

I nod my head yes. That does sound nice, and it could help me relax a bit.

When we finish opening presents, I help my mom pick up the wrapping paper from the living room and clean up the kitchen from breakfast. I head up to my room and put away my new clothes and grab a bag out of the closet to pack for Jeremiah's. I toss in a pair of pajamas, an outfit for tomorrow, some makeup, and a toothbrush. Oh, and clean underwear . . . can't forget those. This will be the first night that I spend with a boy, and I'm nervous but excited. Truthfully, I think I'm more nervous about meeting Jeremiah's dad.

I hope he likes me.

After I'm packed and ready for Miah to pick me up, I take a little time to put more music on my iPod. I give Taylor a call to ask how her Christmas is going and if she got any good gifts, but she spends most of the conversation trying to convince me to add lingerie to my bag for tonight. The rest of the call is me objecting, telling her that his dad and sisters will be in the rooms next to us. Besides, I don't even own any lingerie...

Once I'm done upstairs, I join my mom on the couch in the living room. We spend the next few hours watching *Home Alone* and stuffing our faces with Christmas cookies that my mom got from a coworker.

The doorbell rings and I jump from the couch as I realize that Miah is here to pick me up. I make a mad dash for the door, swinging it open to find him standing with a beautifully wrapped present in his hands and a wide smile on his face. It started snowing while my mom and I were watching the movie, and the flakes are sticking to his slicked-back black-and-pink hair. Some flakes are stuck to his long, dark lashes too. He's my favorite present today, nothing can compete... not even a brand-new iPod.

He enters the house and wraps his arms around me, still holding the present, and lifts me off the ground. With a soft kiss, he whispers in my ear, "Merry Christmas, Little Jetta," and then he carefully places my feet back on solid ground.

"Mmmmm, merry Christmas, Jeremiah," I reply, with my hands still wrapped around his neck.

My mom turns the corner and makes her way into the front hallway. "Don't make me regret allowing you two to spend the night together," she says nervously.

I turn and roll my eyes at her.

Miah reaches out with the present in his hand, offering it to my mom. "I saw this and thought you might like it. I'm not the best at gift giving, but I try." My mom smiles at Miah and slowly takes the present from him.

"Thank you, this is really kind of you."

"Don't thank me yet. You could hate it," Miah says with a small chuckle.

Miah and I stand next to each other as she unwraps her present and opens the box inside. She pulls out a coffee mug and turns it in her hand as she admires it. Then she holds the mug to her chest and looks up at Miah with a sincere smile and tears in her eyes. I look at my boyfriend, wondering what in the world he could have given her to make her cry...

"This is lovely. The perfect gift." She leans in and hugs Miah with the box and mug still in her hands.

When they are done hugging, she turns to me and hands me the mug. It's white ceramic with a Christmas scene printed on it and a quote that reads, "Faith is believing in things when common sense tells you not to." Passing the mug back to my mom, I look over to Miah.

"How did you know that *Miracle on 34th Street* is her favorite movie?" I ask him.

"Oh, she mentioned it when we were chatting once, while I waited for you to get ready." My heart turns to mush thinking of how thoughtful this guy is.

"For someone who is self-conscious about gift giving, this is pretty good." I laugh at him and kiss him on the cheek before I run upstairs to grab my bag.

We say goodbye and goodnight to my mom and head out to Miah's dad's house.

On the way, he fills me in on how Angie has been since she got home. He mentions that she has been distant toward everyone and hasn't spoken much. Evie has scheduled an abortion for Angie on January third. Miah and Evie plan to go with her for support and to take care of her afterward. I ask him how Angie feels about everything, and he says she didn't say a word. I don't know what she's experiencing, but it can't be easy. It's heartbreaking to think she has been going through most of this alone—she must be feeling really scared. I hope Miah and Evie comfort her and reassure her that she's not alone.

CHAPTER TWELVE

Santa Baby

Miah turns down a long driveway and parks the car close to the garage. He pops open the trunk as he jumps out of the driver's seat. We both grab items from the trunk—I take a box of wrapped presents and my overnight bag, and he carries his backpack and his own bundle of gifts—and make our way to the house. Miah opens the front door and leads me inside. I first spot Evie sitting on a long couch next to the Christmas tree in the living room. She's holding a coffee cup between her hands, and I can see fluffy white marshmallows peeking over the brim. As soon as we enter the living room, she places the mug on the coffee table in front of her and leaps up off the couch. Evie embraces me in a tight hug, and I go limp with my arms dangling at my sides.

"Merry Christmas! You're finally here!" she squeals. I am not one for hugs, so I gently place my arms around her back, giving her a few pats. Over her shoulder, and across from where I'm standing, I see a girl with long blond hair sitting on a large, floral-patterned upholstered armchair. Leaning on one of the weathered armrests, she looks a little older than me but not by much, and her attention seems lost in whatever is on the TV in front of her.

"Merry Christmas, Evie. Good to see you again," I say. Evie takes a step back and I smile at her. She jabs her elbow into Miah's stomach.

"Merry Christmas, Bro."

"Bah, humbug," Miah says with a chuckle.

"Did Jeremiah tell you he doesn't like Christmas? He hates the pressure of buying gifts for people." Evie rolls her eyes and looks over at me.

Before I can answer, a faint voice comes from behind her. "Merry Christmas. You must be Cora." Evie moves out of the way to reveal the blond-haired girl I saw sitting in the chair now standing to greet me.

"That's me . . . You must be Angie?"

"That's me," she says with a small laugh.

She's tall, almost as tall as Miah, but that's about the only physical trait the two of them have in common. She's thin, but it looks like a sickly thin. Her hair doesn't share a pink streak like her sister's and brother's, but it drapes down almost to her hips. Angie's eyes are green with large dark bags under them, making me think she hasn't had proper sleep in a long time.

Once our interaction is over, she gives a meek smile and saunters out of the room, and I just watch her go. When I snap back to reality, I realize that Evie and Miah have moved from beside me and are unloading the presents Miah and I brought, placing them under the tree. I join in, until I hear a loud, booming voice behind us.

"Hey, JJ!" Miah and I both turn to see a tall middle-aged gentleman with broad shoulders, black shoulder-length hair, and a dark beard standing before us. I can see glimpses of tattoos on both of his arms from underneath the rolled-up sleeves of his flannel shirt. He looks like a giant lumberjack. Miah steps toward him and they hug each other tightly, slapping each other's backs. The giant man turns to me and embraces me in a hug. I return the gesture, but I can barely breathe from how strong he is.

I'm really over all this hugging . . .

"Cora! So nice to finally meet you. I'm John, JJ's dad. I've heard so much about you and those eyes!" He turns to Miah, "You're right, they are beautiful, Son." I can feel the heat flushing my cheeks and all the way to the tops of my ears.

Miah laughs as he takes my hand in his and kisses my knuckles. He knows I get embarrassed by compliments, but his touch eases my discomfort.

"Come, Cora, sit and relax. What can I get you to drink?" John asks, waiting for my answer as he stands in the doorway separating the living room from the kitchen.

"I'll take a water, please. Thank you," I politely say and smile.

"Be right back. Make yourself at home. I hope you're hungry because we are eating in about twenty." I nod my head in response, still smiling. With the last of the presents tucked under the tree, Miah and I settle onto the couch.

"Your dad is so energetic. I love his enthusiasm," I whisper to Miah.

He laughs at me. "Yeah, I guess I didn't get that from him."

"No, you definitely did, or you wouldn't be a musician who performs on stage in front of a ton of people." I lean over and kiss his cheek, feeling the warmth there as, for once, *he* blushes at *my* comment.

John returns with drinks for Miah and me and joins us on the couch. We chat for twenty minutes about school, work, life, basically everything. We continue the conversation at the dinner table while we eat a delicious Christmas turkey with all the fixings. During the meal, I notice Angie doesn't say much. She did chime in with a comment or a giggle here and there, but that was about it.

When we finish dinner, everyone helps clear the table and get the kitchen back in order. Once the cleaning is complete, we all gather around the Christmas tree as John hands out presents to everyone. I got John, Angie, and Evie each a unique handblown glass ornament as a thank-you for having me for Christmas. The three of them have never seen anything like the glass orbs, and they all seem very appreciative and amazed.

It's such a cool experience to watch the Novak siblings open their presents together on Christmas. I've never had this in my life, and I always wondered what it would be like. I can't stop watching them in amazement. To me, it's like living in the desert and seeing snowflakes for the first time. I'm so in awe of the way they joke and mess around, but also how they are so kind and grateful for each other. These are the moments when I wish I had a sibling to bond with. Someone who could be with me throughout my life, and we could lean on each other when times get hard . . . like if our parents were getting a divorce. I do have Taylor, and to me, she is as close to a sister as you can get without the blood relation. That makes me lucky enough.

Miah and I head upstairs after the presents are all

unwrapped and we have gorged ourselves on cookies and pie. John left Miah's childhood bedroom the same in case he ever needed to move back home. The walls are painted dark blue, almost black, which is so fitting for him—much more appropriate than the light-blue room at his current house. There are tons of band posters tacked up, and the photographs on the walls aren't of his family but of friends I've never met. Some of the pictures are of The Restrictions performing for small crowds.

On Miah's desk sits a framed photo of him with his mom, and he looks about five years old. Tears sting my eyes knowing that in ten years, that little boy will lose his mom. Claire was beautiful. She had blond hair and topaz eyes, just like Jeremiah's. A large, brilliant smile is stretched across her face. I touch the photo with my finger, as though I can soothe the impending pain and sadness for either of them.

My eyes move to a small shelf above the desk, and my hand follows, touching a blue dog collar with a gold tag resting on a cream-colored box with black paw prints painted along it. I delicately lift the dog tag to read what the inscription says: "JINGLES." I push up onto my tiptoes when I notice there's writing on the top of the box. In cursive is a poem called "The Rainbow Bridge." At the end of the poem, it reads: "Our Beloved Jingles (1997–2005)." During the past couple of months with Miah, I had forgotten about Jingles, the dog Claire had gotten the family before she passed away. I stand back, looking between the box that holds Jingles's ashes and the photo of Jeremiah and Claire. Sadness overwhelms me like a dark rain cloud hovering above me.

Pushing away the grief that's crept into my thoughts and

focusing again on the band posters on the walls, I say, "I like teenage Miah's décor. This paint color is awesome." Miah stops fixing the bed and winks at me.

"Are you being a brat, Little Jetta?"

"No, I'm being serious!" Miah walks over and snatches me up by the legs as I squeal. He gently tosses me onto the bed. He tickles my sides, but I can't even tell him to quit it because I'm laughing so hard. When I get the hiccups, he stops and crawls over top of me. Miah stares into my eyes and I stare into his as a hiccup escapes from me every now and then. He leans in and kisses my neck, and I close my eyes. The heat from his kiss travels through my body and sits between my thighs. I suddenly forget I have the hiccups, or they went away—I'm not sure nor do I care.

"You're lucky we are guests in my dad's house, or I'd be punishing you for making fun of me," he whispers in a sultry tone in my ear. He softly kisses my lips. When he starts to move away, I grab his shirt and pull him back to me. Our lips crash, and we kiss each other hard while my hips thrust into him, wanting more.

He slowly moves away and looks at me through hooded eyes. "I would love to give you that present tonight, but I have this thing about doing that in the house I grew up in with family in the other room." Understanding, I nod my head. I would be so embarrassed if they were to hear us.

Miah gets off the bed and walks over to the backpack he brought and pulls out a small box. It's wrapped in silver paper with a small hot-pink bow on top. He takes the handful of steps back to the bed and offers me the gift. I look up at him, noticing he has a sheepish smile on his face.

"What's this?" I ask.

"Well, take it and open it." He jiggles the box in my face for me to take it, so I do.

"A pink bow, huh? Not black or gray?" I tease.

"Nah, you're not a black or gray kinda gal, Little Jetta."

I snicker and begin to carefully unwrap the present. Under the silver paper is a rectangular white box. I open the lid to find a necklace, which causes me to let out a small gasp. I take the necklace out of the box and hang it from my fingers to get a better look. Dangling from a delicate silver chain is a dark-green emerald gemstone cut in the shape of a teardrop.

"The emerald symbolizes truth and love," he says while he watches me study the gem.

"Jeremiah, it's stunning. I love it."

"I want you to be able to carry me with you when I'm touring. I want you to remember that I'll always love you and be truthful." I stop looking at the necklace to shift my gaze to Miah. He's nervously waiting for my reaction. I hand him the necklace and stand up. Knowing what I'm wordlessly asking him to do, he takes it and opens the clasp as I turn and brush my hair to the side. Miah carefully places the necklace around my neck and fastens it. He kisses my shoulder before he turns me around to face him.

Admiring the jewel, I confess, "Miah, this is the best gift I've ever received." I look up at him and place a gentle kiss on his lips. "You are amazing at giving gifts, by the way. Christmas should be your favorite holiday moving forward." He laughs and rolls his eyes at me.

I make my way over to my overnight bag on the floor by the door, and I pull out the gift I got Miah. We both sit down on the bed and turn toward each other as I hand him the present.

"You didn't have to get me anything," he says as he takes it from me.

I shrug. "I love giving gifts, it's my favorite thing about Christmas."

He stops opening the package and looks up at me through his dark lashes with a playful grin.

"What are you thinking, JJ?" I say, squinting my eyes.

"I'm thinking that's very you. You're too kind, but I like it. Please don't change. There aren't enough kind people in the world anymore," he says as he continues to open his gift. "I also see you are wondering about the nickname 'JJ.' Jeremiah John Novak. My mom and dad are the only ones who call me JJ."

"It's cute . . . catchy." I like it. I really do, but I won't use a nickname his mom used. It seems sentimental to him, and I respect that.

"Cora, this is spot on!" Miah says, holding my gift in his hands as he stares at it in awe.

A couple of weeks ago, I started messing around with one of my dad's old film cameras he left at the house, prepping myself for my photography class next semester. I ended up taking a bunch of photos of The Restrictions at one of their recent shows. It was an important gig for the guys because they were opening for a big-time pop/punk band.

I was developing the prints in my school's darkroom when I came across the perfect shot of the band while they performed. All four members had their heads up and hands in the air, singing along with the crowd. The photo looked awesome in black and white, and I knew Miah would love it because the last time I went to his house, I noticed he had no recent pictures of the band in his room. I framed the black-and-white shot and included some other prints in my Christmas gift.

"Holy shit, you are rad at this. Can I get the film for these so we can use them on our MySpace and website?" I nod my head yes while I bite my lip.

Miah takes my hand and we rise from the mattress to stand facing each other. He holds my face with his hands. "Perfect. You're perfect, Cora. Thank you so much."

"Mmmm, nah—" But before I can continue to protest, he kisses me and I kiss him right back.

* * *

I wake up feeling like I'm floating on a cloud. Spending the night with Jeremiah was serene and addicting, and I hope we can do it again soon. Thinking about it, I didn't get that much sleep. I spent the first couple of hours in bed being so excited to lie next to him and feel him close all night that I ended up talking his ear off. Miah fell asleep before me while I was chatting, so I spent another hour watching him peacefully sleep and wondering what he was dreaming about, or if he was even dreaming at all.

My body has an internal alarm clock because of school, so I automatically wake up at seven o'clock . . . even on weekends and holidays. Not wanting to leave Miah yet, I lie there until my stomach growls and I can't wait for food any longer. Slipping out of bed so as not to wake him, I quietly get dressed and head downstairs.

When I enter the kitchen, I notice Angie is sitting at the table by herself. She's reading a book, so I silently move through the room and over to the coffee pot, not wanting to interrupt her. I pour myself a cup of coffee and add cream and sugar, which are at the ready next to the pot. John laid out fruit salad, muffins, donuts, scones, and a bunch of other breakfast pastries and breads like a buffet. I snatch a blueberry muffin from the counter, scoop some fruit into a bowl, and take a seat at the table across from Miah's sister. I poke at a grape while I look around the kitchen, trying to avoid focusing too long on Angie. As I'm about to take a bite of my muffin, Angie closes her book and places it on the table in front of her.

"I'm not going through with the abortion, you know," Angie states.

I put down my muffin and look over at her with wide eyes. I'm unsure of what to say. I just stare back at her, hoping she says something else or nothing at all so that I don't have to respond.

"I know you know, and I need your help convincing Jeremiah that I want to keep the baby." She gets up and sits down in the chair right next to me.

"Angie, I don't think it's a good idea for me to get involved," I finally reply.

"Please, you're the only chance I have." Her hands are clasped together on the table in front of her, like she's praying for me to say yes. I look into her eyes and see that she doesn't want to go through with this. My heart breaks thinking of the women who have had to make this decision in their lives.

"I will talk to him—*with you*. But, Angie, I don't think your brother needs convincing. He told me it's been a long time since you two have really talked, and I don't know if you realize how much he cares about you. My bet is that he's going to say it's your choice since it's your body."

A grimace flashes across her face. "I know, but I don't have anyone, ya know? My friends at school would bail if they knew—they aren't even my real friends. And Evie and I never talk anymore. We are so different." She shrugs her shoulders and touches her palm to her belly. "I just feel really alone. I don't even know who the dad is. It was such a stupid mistake. But maybe I'm supposed to be a mom. I do know that I'm ready to find out."

I watch Angie as she looks down at her belly—which hasn't even developed the slightest bump yet—with a smile and love in her eyes. Seeing her, I realize that she and I both know what it feels like to be alone. "I will help you talk to Miah. I honestly don't think you even need to, but if you want to include him in your decision, then let's do it." I place my hand on hers that's resting on her belly. I don't even know Angie, but she is Miah's sister, so she's my family too.

"I dropped out of school and I'm moving back home. I told my dad, and he's so happy I'm coming home. I just want to do what's right. I want to be a mom—but more than that, I want to be a *good* mom . . . like mine was." Tears slip down her cheeks, but she's still smiling.

"You will be. This will all work out. You have an amazing family here to help you."

She drops her head as she whispers, "Thank you."

Just then, I hear footsteps on the stairs. Miah stops in the doorway to the kitchen and looks between Angie and me. Angie wipes her face with the palms of her hands and clears her throat as she looks up at me.

"What's going on? Is everything okay?" Miah asks as he walks toward us. I look at Angie and then back to Miah, waiting to see if she says anything.

"Jeremiah, Angie wants to talk to you about something." Miah closes the distance between us, and I stand. I take Miah by the hand and gesture for him to take the seat I was just sitting in.

"Okay...," he says, staring at his sister.

Angie stares back at him, and I think she's building courage. After several moments, she finally speaks.

"I'm keeping the baby."

Miah looks up at me and then back to Angie.

"Oh gosh, yes," Miah sighs with relief. "Angie, if you want to have this baby, we are all for it. Why would you make a big deal out of telling me? I'm sad that you think I would judge you or some shit. I love you. You need to understand that it's *your* baby and *your* body. Don't let me or anyone else tell you what you can and cannot do."

Angie smiles at me and then turns back to Miah. Still sitting, she lunges at him and hugs him tightly. "I'm sorry, Jeremiah. I'm just really scared and lost." They are still hugging as Angie begins to cry again.

"I know, Ange. We are going to get through this." He gently pushes her back into her seat, holding her shoulders as he places his forehead to hers. "Now eat something... You need to eat and take care of yourself and that baby."

Angie nods her head and stands up. She heads toward the food on the counter and starts fixing herself a plate.

Miah turns to face me and smirks. I step toward him and sit on his lap, placing my arms around his neck.

"Well, good morning to you," he purrs as he leans in and places a kiss on my lips.

"Mmmm, good morning. I couldn't wait for you to wake up, my stomach was eating itself." Miah laughs and we stand up together.

"Thanks for talking to Angie. I feel bad that she thought I would disapprove. Evie and I scheduled the procedure only because she originally had asked us to," Miah whispers to me.

"I know, Miah, you don't need to defend or explain yourself. How exciting, though! You're going to be an uncle!" I say as I bounce up and down on my tiptoes, and I hear Angie giggle from the kitchen counter.

We spend the rest of the day with Jeremiah's family, looking at old photos from when the Novak siblings were younger. We talk about the baby, and Angie tells us names she's been thinking of. Miah told Angie she can turn his room into a nursery, and she was over the moon about it. She asked Miah and me to help her decorate and put together the furniture with her.

Being involved in Angie's pregnancy makes me feel like I'm starting to form a family of my own. One that I never had the privilege to experience growing up. It makes me feel like I have somewhere I belong and people I can count on even though I've only just met them for the first time.

CHAPTER THIRTEEN

WTF, Kayla?

February 2006

Taylor turns down the music as we pull into a parking spot outside the mall. Besides driving to school when she has to, it's rare that Taylor uses her own car mostly because she hates how old and beat-up it is. Her mom forced her dad into buying Taylor a rusted-out purple 1995 Geo Tracker because it was "safe." It's the kind of car whose heat only works when your foot is on the gas, and the seats are so uncomfortable because the springs have begun to pop through the cushions. I felt guilty that Taylor was stuck with her Geo Tracker when my parents gifted me with my Jetta, but when she saw my car for the first time, she was more excited than I was. She just kept jumping up and down, repeating aloud, "Thank you, God, for giving Cora cooler parents than mine!"

Unfortunately, she's stuck with the task of driving us to the mall tonight. I met Taylor at her place after school, and when her mom got home from work, she blocked me in the driveway. She was busy with a lingering work call, and Taylor and I decided it was best not to interrupt her as we were trying to leave, and so we were forced to take Taylor's car.

It's the first Monday of February, and Taylor and I haven't seen much of each other lately since we've both been busy with our boyfriends. She demanded that we take a trip to the mall to get something "sexy" for Valentine's Day. I'm dreading this because sexy is not my thing. Plus, I don't think I need anything to make my relationship sexier... I'm still new at this, and Miah doesn't have a problem with my brand of sexiness, but I go along with it for Taylor.

"Girl, I'm telling you, just get some cute underwear for the night. Feel good about yourself—do something wild, Cora!" I blush and hop out of the car.

We cross the parking lot and enter the mall. Victoria's Secret is busy with customers searching for Valentine's Day gifts, no doubt. As we browse the lingerie, Taylor chats about all the stuff we need to do before she leaves for the University of Maine in August. The start of her fall semester feels like years away, but I know it will come up quickly. I tell her how things are going with Miah, and I fill her in on how Angie and the baby are doing. Since Christmas, Angie has moved back to Portland, and she and I have become closer.

Taylor and I start discussing my birthday next month and how we should celebrate, as I'll legally be an adult. Turning eighteen doesn't mean much to me, and neither do birthdays in general anymore, but Taylor likes to celebrate... everything.

"Okay, how about we grab dinner and then go to a concert?" she offers.

"Hmmmm, I can agree to that." I pluck a purple lace bra with matching panties off the rack and wiggle the hanger in front of me. Taylor laughs and snatches it out of my hands.

"I'm getting these for you."

"No! Seriously, don't waste four hundred dollars on that. I could just wrap some shoelaces around me and call it sexy." I overexaggerate the cost a bit, but seriously, who pays eighty-five dollars for something resembling gift ribbon? It's a waste of money in my mind, but I do enjoy browsing the store. Maybe someday I will like lingerie . . .

Taylor pulls me back to reality when she calls my name. "Cece, I'm buying them, and you will wear them." She turns on her heels and makes a beeline for the counter. When she's done checking out, she turns to me laughing and tosses the purple number at me. Embarrassing myself, I manage to awkwardly catch it.

Where the heck am I going to hide this from my mom?

* * *

After our shopping trip, we grab a pizza and drive back to Taylor's house to watch a movie. She and I spend the rest of the night eating, chatting, laughing, and sometimes paying attention to the movie. During one of the rare moments we are intently watching a dramatic scene, Taylor suddenly jumps up off the bed.

"Okay, I was going to wait until it was closer to your birthday to give this to you, but I don't want you to make other plans with anyone else." She walks to the desk in the corner of her room, opens a drawer, and pulls out a white envelope. With an excited spring in her step, she prances back over to where I'm sitting on the bed and hands me the envelope.

"What's this?" I ask her as I take it.

"Open it," Taylor says with a smirk.

I peel open the envelope, and inside are four concert tickets to see Paramore in Boston.

"OH MY GOD!" I shout. "Taylor, I love you so much!" I jump up and hug her. Excitement floods me and I begin to hop up and down on my toes, squealing shamelessly, and Taylor joins in.

"You're welcome! I asked Miah for some hints on what to get you and he let me know you've been talking about seeing Paramore for a while now. Lars and Miah are coming with us too."

"This is such an awesome gift, truly. Thank you." I hold the tickets in my hands and rub my thumbs against them, as though I have to check that they're real and not a figment of my imagination. We immediately start planning our outfits for the concert and toss around ideas for where to grab dinner in Boston beforehand.

Coming down from the high of Taylor's amazing gift, I realize I'm starting to get tired. I put the tickets in my bag and make myself comfortable in Taylor's bed. She climbs in too and snuggles in next to me while the movie keeps playing. Eventually, we drift off to sleep.

* * *

We both sit bolt upright at the sound of Taylor's alarm going off in the morning. I forgot that it's a school day, but I lie back down to mentally prepare myself to get out of bed for the day. I stay there for a few minutes and then finally convince myself to crawl out from under the covers. While Taylor is in the shower, I get ready in her bedroom, using her vanity mirror.

Once we are all set to go, we drive to school in our own cars. It's Tuesday, and Taylor has basketball after school, so I take my Jetta to go straight home when school's over. After parking next to each other, we hustle into the building through the student entrance just as the first bell rings. I wave to Taylor and rush down the hall to get to my marine biology class. There's no need to rush, but I do anyway. Even though I'm only taking three classes this semester and I don't need any of them to graduate, they've been pretty enjoyable so far—who would have thought I'd actually take an interest in schoolwork? Plus, I really like my marine biology teacher, Mrs. Brooks. She makes the class fun and puts a lot of effort into teaching . . . I feel like she deserves my respect to at least show up on time.

I enter the classroom and plop down in my seat next to Kayla McKinnon. Kayla is a popular girl who jumps from friend group to friend group. I don't hate Kayla, but I definitely could go without overhearing her and Sarah, who sits on the other side of her, talk about all the boys they met over the weekend. It makes me feel uncomfortable listening to her talk shit about guys, some of whom I know, as if they are the dumbest creatures on earth when in fact, most of them are genuinely nice and don't deserve to be insulted, especially by Kayla McKinnon. To make matters worse, Kayla and Taylor hang out sometimes. They met through the field hockey team and occasionally spend time together outside school. When asked, I kindly turn down invitations from Taylor to hang with her and Kayla. I'm all set, thanks.

I pull out my notebook from my cross-body satchel, and as I'm bending to set my bag next to me on the floor, I sense Kayla's eyes on me. I sit back in my seat and look to the front of the classroom, but she doesn't stop staring at me so I turn and meet her gaze.

"Are you dating that guy Jeremiah from that, like, punk band?" she finally blurts out.

"Umm, yeah. The band is called The Restrictions."

"Whatever. So, like, really weird, but I met him a few weeks ago and he friended me on MySpace. I posted a new profile photo the other night and your boyfriend liked it and commented, 'nice.' If you ask me, it's pretty creepy since he's older but, like, also, he has a girlfriend. Which happens to be you . . . apparently."

I'm so angry that I have to look away from her. My blood is boiling all the way up into my face. My hands are immediately sweaty as I twirl a pen between my thumb and index finger.

Who does Kayla think she is? He would never . . . Or would he? Remember to trust him, Cora. She's such a bitch . . . "Apparently"?

I tell myself to take five deep breaths to calm myself down. Once I've got my emotions under control again, I will respond nicely because I'm not Kayla McKinnon . . . Thank God for that.

Breathe.

"I wouldn't know whose photos he likes on MySpace.

It's not like I track his every move. Plus, maybe he was just trying to be nice, since he's a nice guy," I fire back without even turning to look at her.

I keep my eyes focused on Mrs. Brooks as she goes on about the zones of the ocean. I know them all, but that's not important right now. Even if I tried to listen to Mrs. Brooks, I can't make sense of what she's saying because all I can hear is my heart beating in my ears. But I do hear Kayla reply with a disgusted "ICK." Out of the corner of my eye, she turns back toward the chalkboard, almost pissed off that I didn't engage more. I'm happy I didn't.

The rest of the class goes by in a blur. I can't focus on anything happening around me. My thoughts are consumed by what I will say to Miah when we talk next, and what his reasoning could possibly be for commenting on Kayla's photo. My eyes sting with the effort of holding back tears. She might be hotter than me and accustomed to always getting the guy, but I don't want Kayla to win this war. Jeremiah is different . . . at least, I thought he was.

Once the bell rings, I realize I never came up with a plan of how to approach this with Miah. I grab my stuff and leave the classroom. I keep walking, exiting the school building. I'm not staying here for the rest of the day. I race home and head straight upstairs to my bed. I peel back the comforter and climb underneath, then I pull it over my body and above my head. I forget about the plan to make a plan. I can't think anymore when the tears start flowing and my head hits the pillow.

Over the next forty-five minutes of sobbing under the covers, I take stock of everything going wrong in my life.

I'm crying because of Jeremiah. I'm crying because of my parents. I'm crying because of how lost I feel about my future. Stuck in a downward spiral, I start hyperventilating and can't catch my breath. The side of my head and my hair are wet from the tears that have seeped into my pillow. My nose won't stop running, but I don't even care, I just keep wiping it with the sleeve of my shirt. A migraine begins to form, and I know I should stop wallowing and gather myself together, so I do. By the time I gain control of my breathing, I've started to drift off to sleep and I just let it happen.

* * *

"Cora, honey?" My body is shaking, and I feel a hand on my arm. I open my eyes to find my mom sitting on the edge of my bed. Looking up at her, I realize that I must have been asleep for most of the day if she's home from work now. Her eyebrows are pinched together as she looks at me with concern. "Hey, sweetie, are you feeling okay?"

I rub my eyes and sit up. The migraine is still there. "I don't want to talk about it." I sigh and fall back onto my pillow.

My mom remains on the bed next to me. She doesn't say anything, and I can tell she's trying to think of how to approach this. She's not dumb; she knows it's about Miah.

"You don't have to tell me, but whatever happened, I'm sure you two will work it out. Just promise me, Cora, if you are unhappy or if he's treating you badly . . . promise me you will not put up with his crap?"

I contemplate whether or not I should tell her what

Kayla said Miah did, but I decide to wait until I can speak to my boyfriend to get his side of the story. I nod my head to acknowledge my mom's request. She gets up and slowly walks to the door, looking at me over her shoulder before she slips into the hallway and gently closes the door behind her.

I sit up again and grab my phone out of my satchel. I have a few missed calls from Taylor and several unread texts from Miah. I debate if I should call Taylor to get her advice first or quit stalling and talk to Miah to get this off my chest.

Before I involve either of them, I decide I'm doing some investigating. I grab my laptop that's on my desk, sit back down on the bed, and flip it open. I log in to MySpace and search for Kayla McKinnon. When she pops up, I click on her profile. I see the recent selfie she posted and click it to view the likes. Sure enough, Jeremiah Novak liked her photo and commented. "Nice!" he'd written.

I suddenly feel sick to my stomach.

I take a good, hard look at the photo. She holds the camera above her head, angled to see not only her face but also the exposed cleavage in her tank top that has something written across the chest. Kayla's long black hair is straightened so the layers perfectly frame her face. She wears dark eyeliner and a flawless face full of makeup.

So, she wasn't lying.

Before I have time to think about what I'm doing, I snatch my cell phone off the bed. I aggressively flip it open, find Miah's name, and forcefully hit the call button. I tap my fingers on my leg as I wait for him to answer.

"You okay?" Miah probes as soon as he answers.

"Umm, yeah." My tone is flat, and I can't hide the sliver of anger that hangs onto my words.

"You don't sound okay. I've been texting you all day and you haven't responded," he replies warily.

"I'm just going to get this over with. A girl from my school, Kayla McKinnon, informed me that she met you at a show a few weeks ago. Said you friended her on MySpace, liked her profile photo, and commented 'nice' on it. I investigated it and sadly, she wasn't lying. Wanna explain yourself, or should I just assume there are other seventeen-year-old girls that you are talking to and seeing behind my back?" I snap at him. I don't realize that I've raised my voice.

"Whoa, Cora. You can't just accuse me of cheating on you from a liked photo and a comment on MySpace, of all places."

"Then please, explain yourself."

"I will," he grits out. "Your *best friend*, Taylor, was at the show with this Kelly girl or whatever her name is and introduced her as a school friend of yours and Taylor's. She added *me* on MySpace, and I liked her photo because she was wearing old merch from a band I used to be in."

Now I'm surprised that Taylor introduced them and didn't even tell me. I can't think of what to say next. I'm still upset he even liked the photo and commented at all—he could have ignored it.

"Are you going to say something, Cora? I didn't do anything wrong here."

"You could have just ignored the photo. And why didn't you tell me you met her?"

"Cora, c'mon. Are you really upset about this?" Miah asks in disbelief.

"Yeah, Jeremiah, I am. I'm pissed. I hate Kayla McKinnon.

She's a mean person, and she treated me like shit today trying to convince me that you were into her."

"I'm sorry I didn't tell you. I'm sorry I interacted with her. I will delete her right now, but this is absurd. You should trust me." When he suggests I'm being absurd, it lights another fire of anger inside me. I don't feel like I'm overreacting, but I know that's what he's implying.

"Actually, Jeremiah, just forget it. I don't want to be with an older guy who flirts with younger girls," I snap back.

"Cora, that's not what I'm doing. I love you."

"I don't care. I love you too, Jeremiah, but apparently a bunch of other girls do too, and you have options. Kayla's prettier and her parents aren't fucked up, so you won the lottery with that one." Fuck, I want to cry again. My voice is starting to sound wobbly, but I just want to be brave.

"You know what, Cora? I don't need to sit here and be roped into some high school bullshit. I'm done with this conversation."

I start crying again and the phone goes dead, just like my heart.

I think Jeremiah just broke up with me.

CHAPTER FOURTEEN

Delete My Profile and Delete Myself

I spent the rest of the night in my room. I didn't go downstairs to eat or drink anything. I knew my mom would ask too many questions, so I avoided her at all costs.

Today is a carpool-with-Taylor day, but I'm so irritated with her that I drive straight to school without picking her up. As I'm turning at the end of the hallway to make my way to marine biology, I hear shouting from behind me.

"Hey! Hey! Hey, Cora, wait!!" I know it's Taylor, but I don't stop walking. Not even to glance at her behind me. I try to quicken my pace but her hand lands on my shoulder and lightly pulls me back. I turn around and she's panting and trying to catch her breath. I continue to stare at her, though; I want her to speak first.

"Cora, what the hell? I texted you all night last night and you didn't respond. Then, you don't show up at my house this morning and now you're ignoring me? What the fuck?"

"No, I have a 'what the fuck' for you, Taylor. You brought Kayla McKinnon to The Restrictions' show weeks ago, introduced her to *my* boyfriend, knowing damn well that Kayla preys on guys with girlfriends . . . Then she friends him on MySpace, he likes one of her selfies with a ton of *boob* showing, and now I don't have my boyfriend anymore. I'm not blaming you, but maybe you could have told me that you introduced them and prepped me for the wrath Kayla would unleash to make me jealous! I thought you were my best friend." I go to turn but she grabs my shoulder again.

"Whoa! You do not get to unload your issues on me and act like I created them. I only introduced Kayla and Jeremiah because she was with me and he came and said hi to me, just to be nice. I know what Kayla's like, but it's not my fault that Jeremiah liked her photo and fell for her trap. You shouldn't be mad at me. I'm always here for you. I always give you the benefit of the doubt because of the shit you're going through with your parents, but you know what, Cora? Fuck you, I'm done too. I'm tired of trying to cheer you up and make you happy. Time to find someone else to do that now." Taylor finishes shouting at me, spins on her heels, and storms back down the hallway.

I just lost my best friend too.

I move seats in marine biology class so that I am away from Kayla. I can't bear to sit next to her, knowing I'd constantly be thinking of Miah... and now Taylor. I manage to make it through the rest of the school day without breaking down. I mean, besides once in a bathroom stall, but it was a small breakdown. An easy cleanup. My heart feels empty, and I feel lonelier than I ever have before. I feel like there's nothing left to live for. My best friend is gone, my boyfriend's gone, my parents might as well be gone, I have no future, nothing to look forward to. It's a tough realization, and it hasn't even been a day since my world crumbled and crashed around me.

When I get home from school, I make my way to my room once more to throw myself a pity party. I open the door to find my mom sitting on my bed.

Oh, come on, this day can't get any worse.

"Cora, come sit down, honey." She pats the space on the bed next to her.

I toss my bag to the side as I walk to my bed.

"Mr. Hughes called me today. Said he overheard you and Taylor arguing in the hallway and was concerned. Since he and I have been friends for a long time, he thought he should call and let me know so I could check in with you. He said he didn't like the way you looked today." She takes my hand and looks at me. I'm too ashamed to meet her eyes. I knew people would overhear Taylor and me, but I thought I could hide this from my mom for at least a month or two. "Can you tell me what's going on?"

Tears roll down my cheeks as I nod at her. "It's stupid. Taylor introduced some girl I don't like to Jeremiah at one of his shows. She friended him on MySpace, and he liked a photo of her showing a ton of cleavage and commented 'nice' on it. I got mad at Miah and Taylor, and now I don't have my boyfriend or my best friend." I continue to cry and wipe at the tears as they drip off my chin.

"Miah shouldn't have done that, but honey, maybe he was just trying to be friendly. He loves you. I can tell he does. Taylor didn't do anything wrong . . . That argument was just you still being upset and taking it out on Taylor. You should apologize to her."

"Well, it's too late now, Mom. Plus, I'm not even sure if

I believe him, and it made me jealous . . . Doesn't that say something about me too?" I ask.

"Yeah, it says you are a young girl trying to navigate her first relationship. Trying to figure out how to love herself and someone else," she says. I finally look up at her and realize she may be right. But I meant it when I said it's too late now.

"What should I do?" I never thought I would ask my mom for relationship advice, but here we are.

"Give it some time. Don't be so quick to call him or reach out to him. During that time, try and figure yourself out and learn to love yourself . . . and apologize to Taylor. She's always been there for you. She doesn't deserve this." I don't know how I'll survive not talking to Miah, but I'll try.

"Okay," I say as my mom pats my hand.

"Honey? Remember that night I came in to talk to you about the divorce and you told me that you would be on my side and not your father's?" She lifts my chin and searches my eyes.

"Yeah, I do."

"I feel like I can explain to you why I said 'don't,'" she says with a small sigh. "There are always two sides to every story within a relationship, and most of the time, neither party is completely blameless. So it's pointless to take sides. You just have to love people for who they are. Everyone makes mistakes, Cora." My mom stands up and gives me a quick kiss on the cheek. She heads to the door and turns to face me once more. "Want to come to yoga with me tomorrow night? I'd like to spend some time with you, and it might help take your mind off things."

"Yeah, Ma, I would love that," I answer.

After speaking with my mom, I feel a lot better. I'm still heartbroken, but I don't feel as lonely as I did before. It felt good to talk to her and to have someone guide me through my problems.

I should do this more often.

I decide to listen to my mom and give it time. Even though it feels like my heart will be broken forever. My stomach feels empty, like I have a constant stomachache.

I spend the rest of the night doing homework and trying to stay off MySpace, but I end up checking it three times. I finally stop kidding myself and delete my profile in order to eliminate the urge to scroll through Miah's profile. I draft up a letter to give to Taylor, but I'm not ready to apologize to her just yet. I'm ashamed of how I acted, and I think she needs time too.

※ ※ ※

Three Weeks Later . . .

Valentine's Day has come and gone. My dad stopped by the house to give me flowers and chocolates, and my mom had a teddy bear and candy conversation hearts sitting on the kitchen island for me in the morning before school. Nothing from Jeremiah, since we haven't spoken to each other in weeks. Taylor has been ignoring me in school, and we haven't been carpooling, which sucks. To make matters worse, she's been hanging out with Kayla McKinnon, so I haven't had a chance yet to give her my apology letter.

I've been going to yoga with my mom every week and I'm

running more. Exercising helps free my mind and de-stress. It helps me feel good mentally. My mom and I have been taking cooking classes together and trying out other various activities, and I have to admit that our mother-daughter dates have been a lot of fun.

I've been making a real effort to spend more time with my dad at his condo the past couple of weekends. He gets candy for us and we make popcorn and rent a movie. Though I still haven't met her, my dad has been opening up to me about Anne. I'm trying to keep an open mind, and overall, she actually sounds pretty nice. He asked me about Jeremiah once but hasn't again since I told him we broke up. He seemed oddly happy about it, though it pained me to even say Miah's name.

I still think about Miah every minute of every day. I wonder what he's doing and if he misses me. One night about a week ago, I reactivated my MySpace out of curiosity. The first picture that popped up was of Miah performing at a show with The Restrictions. I studied his face for a moment until that all-too-familiar sickness crept in my stomach again. My body went tense, and a pain struck my heart. I quickly snapped my laptop shut and I haven't looked at MySpace since. Most nights I cry myself to sleep, but I would never tell anyone. I miss Miah so much that it makes me feel hollow. Sometimes I'm not even sure if I'm breathing or blinking because everything feels hazy. Like I'm missing the part of myself that makes everything make sense. I try to find happiness throughout my day to take my mind off him . . . but my thoughts always drift back to his eyes, his smile, the way he smelled, and his voice calling me "Little

Jetta." I pray every day that he will reach out to me; frankly, I can't even remember why I was mad anymore, but I'm just going to leave it be.

"Hey, Cora, wait up!" I hear as I'm leaving school and walking to my car. I turn around and see my friend Kyle jogging toward me.

"What's up, Kyle?" I say when he's in front of me.

"Can you give me a ride home?" he asks.

"Sure, hop in."

We both get in the car, and as I put the key in the ignition and buckle my seatbelt, Kyle starts chatting away about new bands he found that we should listen to. I hear him speaking as I drive, trying my best to pay attention, but I get lost in my thoughts... Kyle loves to talk. *Loves* to talk.

Taylor and I met Kyle at a show about a year ago. He was with a few other people from our school, but we had never met them. Kyle approached us at the show and told us he had seen Taylor around school. Being a couple of grades above him, we hadn't noticed him before. But since then, we've seen Kyle at a bunch of gigs and mingled with him when we could.

Kyle and I started hanging out more regularly a few weeks ago. He's in my photography class, and we were paired up to work on a portrait project together. While working on the assignment, we had a lot of fun and got along really well. It's nice to have a friend—even if he doesn't shut up. It helps that we share the same interests, and one of those interests is not dating each other... at least, it's not an interest I have. I enjoy being his friend, and my heart belongs to someone else, still.

"Wanna hang and have dinner tonight? My mom's making your favorite, Hainanese chickennnn . . . ," Kyle taunts.

Kyle is from Singapore. His parents moved their family to Portland when he was nine due to his dad's job transfer. Kyle talks about Singapore a lot, so much so that I want to visit someday. He says it's beautiful and clean and always warm. I can tell he misses his home, and honestly, judging by the way he reminisces about it, I would too.

"Errr, I gotta head home. My mom and I are going to yoga tonight. Besides, I know that your mom makes Hainanese chicken every Thursday," I tease. "Next week, I'll be there."

I pull up to his house and turn into the winding driveway. Kyle's parents are loaded. I've never asked him what they do, but he has mentioned his dad is in the tech industry. Their house is pretty much a mansion, but he does have three sisters, so I can understand the need for space.

"Awww, man. Okay, but can we hang tomorrow night? Wanna go see *Final Destination 3*!? I've been dying to see it. No pun intended."

I laugh and shake my head. "Yeah, I'm down with that. Remind me tomorrow at school." Kyle smiles widely in response.

He climbs out of my car and I watch him dash up the long stone pathway to the steps of his house. His shoulder-length chocolate-colored hair bobs as he walks. Once he reaches the door, he turns and waves as I shift my car into reverse.

Kyle's a cute kid, and he's like a younger brother to me. I think any girl would be lucky to date him. Not just because he's objectively good looking, with his olive skin tone, copper-colored eyes, and how he's somehow jacked even though he's more of the video gamer type than the fitness or sports type of person. But more than that, Kyle is simply a nice guy. He's sweet, attentive, cultured, and smart. Someday, one girl is going to be very happy.

※ ※ ※

Kyle and I are at the movie theater for the 6:15 p.m. showing of *Final Destination 3*. I'm not a huge fan of scary movies, but the Final Destination series is more suspense than horror. If it had supernatural stuff like demonic possessions, I would have kindly passed. *The Exorcist*? Yeah, not for me.

While we are waiting in line for some snacks at the concession stand, I suddenly see Taylor and Lars in front of us picking up their food and cashing out. I feel embarrassed—not because I'm with Kyle, but because I'm not sure what I should do. Do I say hi? Do I ignore them? I debate on whether or not I should tell Kyle I have to go to the bathroom, but before I can run, Lars spots me and smiles. I look over to Taylor, and she looks back at me but her face is blank with no readable expression. They start walking straight toward us.

Oh, great.

"Hey, Cora! Long time no see!" Lars says as his eyes flick between Kyle and me.

I glance at Kyle and he shrugs his shoulders in response. I already filled him in on what happened between Taylor and me, so I'm sure his shrug was a gesture of "I don't know what to do either."

Thanks, Kyle.

"Hey, Lars, how have you been?" I respond, genuinely curious.

"Good, good. How about you?"

"Good. Busy." I'm hoping this is as far as the conversation goes . . . but I never get what I wish for.

"Hey, would you want to come to our show in a few weeks? It's our last performance at Cal's before they close for good. I know you and Miah aren't talking, but the band misses you."

I grab a strand of hair and mindlessly start playing with it between my fingers. Cal's closing is unfortunate, and I'd love to say goodbye to the grimy dive bar, but I'm not sure I can face Miah and his bandmates yet. "I'll think about it. Thanks for the invite, though."

"Your hair got long," Taylor says, surprising me.

I look at the strand I'm playing with and realize that it has. Instead of landing just above my shoulders, it now rests by my collarbones. I've enjoyed braiding my hair lately, so I haven't been getting it cut, or dyed. The red streaks have faded into amber-colored highlights, and oddly enough, my hair color now resembles my mom's.

I nod my head. "Yeah, I guess it has."

Taylor smiles back at me in response.

"Well, we should grab our snacks and get into the theater." I nearly jump hearing Kyle's voice. I forgot he was standing next to me.

"Oh yeah! Oh shoot!" The realization that Kyle and Lars haven't been introduced hits me. "Lars, this is my friend Kyle. Kyle, this is Taylor's boyfriend, Lars," I say quickly. They both dip their chins in greeting.

"Nice meeting you. And Cora, I hope you make it to the show in a few weeks." Lars and Taylor begin to walk away, toward the theaters. I give them a small wave as they disappear from view.

"Well, that was awkward," I admit to Kyle as we stand at the counter. He just laughs at my comment.

I couldn't focus on the movie. People were screaming from roller coaster accidents and tanning bed misfortunes, but all I could think about was Taylor's remark and how she smiled at me. That was the first time she's smiled at me or even acknowledged me in weeks. I think it's time to give her my apology letter.

When the movie ends, Kyle and I decide to grab a pizza and head back to my place to hang for a bit. While we eat, I fill him in on my plan to apologize to Taylor on Monday morning at school. Kyle is supportive and thinks it's a great idea. It's nothing crazy—just an apology—but I'm nervous about how she will react to my letter . . . so support from a friend is comforting right now.

CHAPTER FIFTEEN

My Heart

Monday morning rolls around quicker than I anticipated. Lately, my weekends have been dragging by without anyone to really hang out with—because visiting my dad doesn't count—but this weekend was different. I've been so eager to give my apology letter to Taylor that Saturday and Sunday were here and gone in the blink of an eye. I decide to arrive at school early, before the first bell, so that I can put my letter in her locker, hoping that no one will see me. Taylor gave me her locker combination years ago in case I ever needed to grab anything from it (like tampons, she had said). I'm not only nervous about Taylor accepting my apology, but I'm also terrible at locker combinations, so this may take me awhile. Admittedly, I struggle with my own locker so much that for the past four years, I've been carrying all my books in my bag or, now that I can drive, leaving some in my car to grab in between classes.

Standing at Taylor's locker, I'm amazed when it only takes me two tries before I hear the loud *click* and the lever pops up to signify it's unlocked. Searching in my bag, I grab a roll of tape and the letter. I quickly rip a piece of tape from the dispenser and place it on the envelope, and then toss the tape back into my bag. The stack of books at eye level seems like the perfect spot to stick the letter so that when Taylor opens her locker, she won't be able to miss it. I slam the locker shut just as students start filling the entrance at the sound of the bell. I close my bag and hustle down the hallway to my marine biology classroom.

I eagerly keep checking my phone throughout my classes, hoping that Taylor will say something before the end of the school day. Truthfully, I don't expect her to accept my apology. What I did was selfish. Taylor has always been there for me, even when no one else was. What happened between Miah and me was not her fault. I should have trusted Taylor... and I should have trusted Miah too.

When my last class of the day is finished, I head out of the school and toward my car. I'm checking my phone again just in case I missed anything while I was in the darkroom during photography class. Still no messages from Taylor. I open my car door and toss my bag in the passenger seat.

"Owww! What the hell!" I hear from inside the car. I duck my head and see Taylor rubbing the side of her arm and my bag lying across the center console.

"Oh my gosh! I'm so sorry, Taylor! What the heck are you even doing in my car?... And how did you get in my car?" I ask, still looking at her through the open door. She waggles her eyebrows and lifts her hand as my spare keys dangle from her index finger.

"You gave me a set the first week you got the car. You said, 'in case of an emergency.'" She snorts and tosses the keys in her bag. I sit down in the driver's seat, close the door behind me, and start the car to warm us up. It's freezing outside, and my fingers were starting to turn blue.

I don't know what to say to Taylor now that she's sitting next to me. I look at her silently with a smirk, waiting to see if she will initiate the conversation.

"Thank you for the letter," she starts. "I didn't mean what I said when I told you that you were selfish. I mean, at the time you were being a tad selfish, but you aren't. You are one of the nicest people I know, and I love you for that."

"You must not know a lot of people . . ." I shrug and chuckle, embarrassed by her compliment.

"No, I do, and no one comes close to my best friend."

"No one comes close to my best friend either. I've been so lost and lonely without you. Kyle's cool, but I can't talk to him about how I feel, or watch rom-coms with him, or go lingerie shopping with him . . . It's not the same without you, Taylor. I'm so sorry."

Taylor laughs, and it startles me a bit. "I know. I'm the best, bitch." She leans over and kisses my cheek. That simple gesture means the world to me. I feel like a weight has been lifted off my chest and I'm able to breathe again.

"All right, tell me all about the sitch with Miah, but like also, give me the deets on Kyle. He's matured quite nicely." I'm just putting on my seatbelt when I freeze and look at her in shock over her Kyle comment. She rolls her eyes and responds, "Lars and I broke up."

"WHAT?! What happened? Are you okay? I legit just saw you guys three days ago." I'm shocked. I thought Lars and Taylor would last for years. They were such a great couple who were always happy and so in love.

"I don't really know what happened. After the movie Friday night, we started talking about the tour in the summer and how I'll be away at college, and I don't know... I guess we both decided it was time to go our separate ways." I'm still looking at Taylor with my eyes wide and mouth agape. "Look, I'm not heartbroken over it, so don't worry about it. I was kind of ready to move on anyway. I missed doing what I wanted to do, and all he wanted to do was practice drums, play drums, dream about drums—it was starting to get old. We were just moving in different directions. At least I was, and he was focused on his music, and that's okay."

I'm finally able to pick my jaw up off the floor and speak. "I'm glad you are okay, because if he hurt you, I would hurt him." Taylor starts laughing.

"How would you hurt him, Cece? Would you give him an evil look? You're too nice to hurt anyone, but thank you for being a good friend."

"Well, apparently, I'm pretty good at hurting people's feelings since I sabotaged two relationships in a matter of two days . . . So there's that." I've started to pull out of the parking lot to drive to Taylor's house. I keep my eyes focused on the road, unsure of what Taylor is thinking in the passenger seat since she's suddenly gone quiet.

"Cece, not for nothing, but Jeremiah really fucking misses you. Maybe you should reach out to him."

"I can't. I was such a bitch. I can't take that back. I blatantly told him I didn't trust him when I should have. The whole thing is stupid."

"Yeah, and by the way, it was torture hanging out with

Kayla, so let's never argue again because I can't stand listening to her talk about how much guys love her. God, she is so full of herself, and she's mean too. Pretty girl but shitty person. It's a shame," Taylor says, shaking her head back and forth.

"I told you so. Kayla McKinnon is a mean girl. She's a Regina George, for sure."

Taylor places her hand on mine that's resting on the gear shift. "I've missed you, Cece."

"I know. I missed you too, Taylor."

When I park at Taylor's, she invites me to come in for a bit to chat more about Jeremiah. I accept the invitation.

It's so nice to have my friend back.

I'm still going to hang with Kyle, but having a girl to talk to again about boy problems and how the breakup has made me feel—it's refreshing.

"So, we need to chat about the Paramore concert this weekend," Taylor announces as she hops onto her bed.

"Oh yeah, I totally forgot!" I say, joining her. Then I second-guess myself and stammer, "If . . . if you don't want to go, I get it."

Please still want to go . . .

"Umm, we are going. For sure. I just need to find two people to come with us, or I could try selling the other two tickets." We both sit in silence, thinking about who we could possibly bring.

"Don't you dare invite Kayla," I warn.

"Don't you dare be stupid. I would never!" She laughs and gently punches my arm. "Hey! What about Kyle and maybe Evie?"

"Eh, Kyle will come. I'm unsure about Evie. I feel like I shouldn't even ask. I'm sure she wants nothing to do with me now that Miah and I aren't together." My heart sinks at the thought of no longer being in contact with Evie and Angie. I wonder how Angie is doing and how far along she is in her pregnancy. I wonder if she's having a boy or a girl. The Novaks are probably so excited. I miss Evie's attitude and honesty, and her dry sense of humor.

Taylor scooches closer to me on the bed and wraps her arm around my shoulders. "What's going on, lady? You okay?" I shake my head and lean on her shoulder.

"I really miss him and his family and being called 'Little Jetta.'" Taylor and I both laugh, but my laugh turns into a small sob.

"Just reach out to Evie and ask her. It would be nice for you to see her," Taylor says.

"You're right. I'll text her tonight."

After a couple of hours catching up on everything we missed in each other's lives from spending three horrible weeks apart, I leave Taylor's house feeling more like myself again. When I get home, my mom is in the kitchen cooking dinner.

Mmmm, smells like tacos.

My stomach growls and I realize I haven't eaten anything since a granola bar earlier this morning when I was heading out the door for school.

My mom turns around when she hears me drop my bag on the ground. "Hey, honey, I'm making fajitas. You hungry?"

"I'm starving! It smells great, Ma." I grab a Diet Coke out of the fridge and take a seat at the kitchen island. I crack open the soda can and watch my mom move around the kitchen, collecting ingredients from the cupboard and fridge.

"Want any help?" I ask her.

"Nah. I'm just finishing up. Just grab a plate and get your tortilla wrap ready with cheese."

"Yes, ma'am." I stand up and do as I'm told.

My mom and I dish our plates and then take our seats at the kitchen island.

"So . . . I saw Jeremiah today," my mom says after her first few bites. I freeze just as I'm about to devour my fajita, holding it above the plate. My heart sinks to my stomach and creates a different kind of fullness. I no longer feel hungry, and I put down my tortilla.

When I don't respond, she continues. "He mentioned that he saw you a couple of weeks ago at a coffee shop with a guy. Said he didn't want to bother you."

"Oh. It was Kyle," I say softly.

A million questions come to my mind. What does his hair look like now? Was he sad? Was he happy? Was he with someone? But I don't ask any of the questions I have sitting on the tip of my tongue. Instead, I wait for my mom to say more. As I wait, I play with the emerald pendant resting against my chest. The necklace Jeremiah got me for Christmas is still latched around my neck. I haven't taken it off since the night he put it on.

"I figured, but I didn't feel like it was up to me to tell him who Kyle was. Jeremiah said he's been busy with band practice and preparing for their tour. He also mentioned that Angie is doing great." My mom pauses again, gauging my reaction but I stay silent. "She's having a boy. He thought you would want to know."

I sit quietly, staring at my plate of food. I'm so happy for Angie, she's probably so excited. I wish I could call her, but I can't.

"He . . . he also asked how you're doing," my mom says with a slight stutter. Almost as if she hesitated to tell me. My heart jumps a bit, knowing that he still does think about me . . . or at least he did when he was talking with my mom. I'm not sure how to respond, maybe I should just not say anything. She knows what happened between us, but I refuse to force his hand. I want to wait until he's ready to talk to me.

"Are you going to say anything?"

"There's nothing to say, Ma. I messed up. When he's ready, he will reach out to me."

She shakes her head at my response. "Eat. Starving yourself won't fix a broken heart, believe me." I do as she says, and I finish my fajita.

Dinner ends in an awkward silence. I help clear the dishes and head up to my room, still sulking. Later that night, I text Kyle about the Paramore concert this weekend and he eagerly agrees to go. After Kyle accepts the invite, I know it's time to reach out to Evie. I falter a moment with my phone in my hand, thinking of what to text her.

Keep it simple. Don't make it seem like you're contacting her for info on Miah.

I type: *Hey, Evie! I hope you're doing well. I miss you! I'm going to see Paramore on Saturday for my birthday and I have an extra ticket. I was wondering if you wanted to come?*

I send the text off quickly so that I can't overthink it and back out. I toss my phone and it lands somewhere on my bed. I don't bother to look as I take a seat at my desk and flip open my laptop. As soon as I press the power button, I hear my phone go off. I pause . . .

Slowly picking up my phone, I see that Evie has responded: *I would love to go! I miss you so much, Cece. Thank you for thinking of me. Just let me know the details Saturday morning.*

A smile stretches across my face reading her response. I can't believe I waited so long to reach out to Evie. Before closing my phone, I reply: *Yay! I'll call you Saturday morning with the deets.*

I slept great that night knowing I would be with my best friends Saturday night, seeing one of my favorite bands. It was almost perfect . . .

If only I had Jeremiah to share my birthday with.

* * *

March 2006

"Happy early birthday!" Evie shouts as she jumps in the backseat of Taylor's car.

My cheeks blush and I smile as I turn to look at her. "Yeah, yeah, thank you."

I've never been a fan of birthdays, and technically mine's not until the eighth, but this one feels different. It's a milestone. I can legally do whatever I want, kind of. Actually, nothing for me will really change. I don't break the rules or go outside the lines of life much at all. I am a pretty damn good kid.

"Get excited, Cora! This is a great birthday," Evie insists. "OH! I got you something." She reaches into her purse and pulls out a small box, then she passes it to me from the backseat. I slowly pull open the wrapping paper and take the lid off the box. Inside sits a thin, silver bangle with a scallop shell placed in the middle. I take the bracelet out and turn it so I can get a better look at the seashell. Carefully painted on the inside of the shell is a beautiful beach scene with sand and blue water. It reminds me of another beach painting I've seen before—it's just like the one in Jeremiah's bedroom.

"This is so pretty, Evie, truly amazing. Thank you so much. Did you get this made?" I ask, still holding the bracelet in my hands.

"Something like that," Evie says with a small giggle. "My mom made it. She loved to paint, and she loved the beach. When she found out she wasn't going to make it, she made Angie and me bracelets for my dad to give us when we turned eighteen. She used to sell her creations, and she just happened to make one extra bracelet—I knew I had to give it to you. She would have loved you."

I carefully put the bracelet around my wrist and close the clasp. My eyes start to burn and I feel the tears accumulating, but I try not to blink and let them fall. Taylor did my makeup for me tonight and I really don't want to ruin it, but this is the sweetest birthday gift I have ever received. Although the scene on the inside of the shell is small, I can tell who taught Jeremiah how to paint.

I shake my head and whisper, "Thank you, Evie." She squeezes my shoulder in response.

"Okay, no more tears! Tonight is going to be fun. SMILE!"

Taylor says as she cranks the dial of the car stereo louder. I turn to see Kyle roll his eyes at Taylor. I sympathize with him being the only boy in the group, but he insisted on coming, so I don't feel that bad for him.

The concert is amazing. We all are having a great time screaming the lyrics and dancing to every song. It is one of the best nights I've ever had. And I catch myself thinking about Miah only once, during the song "My Heart." This week, I've been getting myself pumped up for the concert by listening to Paramore's album on repeat, but I intentionally skipped over that song each time it was about to play. I've started to place restrictions around anything that will remind me of Jeremiah. I'm getting better at keeping my thoughts from drifting to him every day, but I'm not sure if I can completely erase him. Evie is doing me a solid by not bringing up Miah at all tonight, but I see her glance at me during "My Heart." I guess I didn't mask my sadness well enough.

CHAPTER SIXTEEN

Seashells by the Seashore

Jeremiah

I don't even know how long it's been since Cora blew up at me over the stupid MySpace shit. Time has been a blur without her. Sometimes it flies by and sometimes it creeps by slowly, second by second. I fucking hate MySpace to begin with—I only have one to appease my bandmates and keep up with our fans. My comment on Kayla's photo was innocent. I honestly didn't even realize I had met the girl until Cora told me I had. When Kayla's picture popped up on my page, I noticed her tank top was an old Say Goodbye band shirt, so I liked and commented. I didn't know merch was still around from my high school band until I saw her shirt.

To me, it was completely harmless.

At the same time, I can see why Cora is furious and how she wants nothing to do with me. I'm not an idiot and I understand that her trust in others, particularly men, is shot to shit since her dad cheated. I just wish she could see that no other girl could *ever* hold a candle to her.

I handled this whole situation wrong. I should have never hung up on Cora. She probably hates me, and I can't blame her. I don't want to reach out to her, primarily because I want to give her time, but also because I don't even know how to apologize for being such a dick.

Lately I've been trying to preoccupy my mind and keep myself busy to the best of my abilities. My smoking habit has had a substantial uptick since the breakup. At one point, I found myself blowing through a pack every two days, which is disgusting and expensive. It's the only thing that takes the edge off since I feel so wound up all the time. I stopped by my dad's house the other day and Evie made a comment about how gross I smelled, so I decided I should cut back on the cigarettes. Now when the anxiety creeps in and I need a fix, I try popping a mint in my mouth instead, and it kind of helps . . . for a bit.

I've been driving Angie to her doctor's appointments, which have only been a couple so far. The whole family went with her to the anatomy scan appointment when they tell you the sex of the baby—it's a boy. It was a great day for us Novaks. We grabbed lunch after and celebrated. We were all just genuinely happy. I'm so excited to have a nephew soon. I can't wait to teach him how to skateboard, play bass, tune up cars, and paint. Most of all, I can't wait to teach him how to be a kick-ass person, like my mom taught us. I'm not saying I'm perfect, but my mom was.

Angie and I started working on the nursery. We're converting my old bedroom, which is right next to Angie's room, so that will be perfect for her. She won't have far to go in the middle of the night. I repainted the walls for her because I didn't want her inhaling any paint fumes, but she designed the whole thing. She's doing a beachy theme with a surfing vibe, which is looking pretty frickin' dope so far.

As a surprise, on one wall, I painted a beach scene with beige sand that has little white seashells hidden throughout. Dark seafoam-green waves crested in aquamarine blue crash against the sandy shore. I even tucked a little turtle in one corner of the mural because who doesn't love turtles?

Angie was blown away when she saw what I'd painted. She stood in disbelief with her hands covering her mouth. I don't think she spoke for a solid five minutes. When she turned to me, she was quietly sobbing. I walked over to her and hugged her tightly. She returned the hug as she whispered a thank-you in my ear. It was all I needed to hear from her. Truly, I knew she was thanking me for more than just the mural, but she's my little sister and I love her. I would do anything for Angie and Evie. No questions asked and no thank-yous needed.

Work has been hectic because we're nearing the end of the quarter, so I've been working on Saturdays. It helps with taking my mind off Cora . . . and making some extra cash for the band's tour. My company has been really cool with letting me take three months off for the summer. I've saved up so much vacation time and sick time that I'll even have some left over when I return. I had planned on using the rest of my days off to take Cora on a trip somewhere fun and warm during her winter break from college. I imagined her happy, limitless, and glowing on a beach as the two of us ditch the real world for a while. Looks like I'll have to think of other ways to spend my time off.

I spoke to Taylor a few weeks ago when she was hanging out with Lars in our living room. I asked her how Cora was doing, and she informed me that they had also stopped talking to each other since the MySpace debacle. I know Taylor was the only real friend Cora had, and her parents are so self-involved, they probably won't even notice that Cora lost her best friend . . . or that we broke up. It aggravated me that Taylor hasn't checked in on her, even if Cora was a jerk to her. Taylor knows what she's going through at home with her parents and with me—she could check in on her. I got short with Taylor when she told me she hadn't spoken to Cora. Another dick move, I know. I could see it on Taylor's face and hear it in her voice that she truly misses Cora and that this is killing her too. Sometimes I need to learn to tone down the protector in me, but when it comes to Cora, I will probably never learn.

Anyway, we found out that Cal's will be officially closing its doors. Chris said something about the owner—Cal himself—moving out of state and selling, but the people who bought the property want to completely gut the place and remodel it into some swanky steakhouse. That pisses me off because I practically grew up at Cal's. I was there almost every weekend either watching bands perform or playing in a band myself. So for one last hoorah, Cal has organized something he's calling "Calapalooza." The name sounds so fucking stupid, but he's a really nice dude so I'll let it pass. It will be a Saturday of nonstop performances by local bands, including The Restrictions.

Lars told me he ran into Cora at the movie theater recently, and he invited her to Calapalooza. He said she didn't seem that into the idea, responding to his invite by shrugging her shoulders and telling him she would think about it. I'm hoping she shows up. I want to see her eyes glowing from the lights beaming off the stage. I want to see that smirk on her face, the one she has when she watches me play knowing that she's mine and I'm hers. I want to see her bite her lip to try to hide a full smile. That hidden smile is Cora knowing damn well that she gets me all to herself after our set, and all night if she wants.

If I get her back, this breakup shit will never happen again.

Lars also mentioned that when he saw her, she was with that kid again. The same kid I saw her with at that coffee shop Grinder's a few weeks ago. I knew it wouldn't be long until another guy swooped in. When I saw them together at Grinder's, they were grabbing their coffees from the pickup counter. He said something to her, and she threw her head back laughing. I envied him. I miss her laughing with me and giving me love-punches on the shoulder . . . which actually really fucking hurt because she's stronger than she realizes. My heart sank when I saw her with him, and a lump formed in my throat. She was just as beautiful as the last time I saw her. Cora looked like she was doing well, considering the drama with Taylor. I wanted to talk to her, but how could I when she looked so happy without me? Besides, I'm not a dummy; this kid is good looking and obviously funny. He seems perfect for her.

I keep thinking about how Cora will be eighteen soon, and I wish I could give her a gift. I had the perfect thing in mind, but I knew I would never be able to get it to her. An idea came to me when Evie texted me the other night letting me know that she would be taking my spot at the Paramore concert for Cora's birthday. She wanted to know if I was okay with her seeing Cora, and I told her that it would be great. I know she loves both of my sisters, and I would never want to take them away from her. Evie asked if I could give her some birthday present ideas for Cora and, after careful consideration, I told her I knew exactly what to get. She would just have to swing by during the week to grab it.

I remembered that on my eighteenth birthday, my dad had given me a bracelet that my mom had made. It was a silver bangle with a seashell in the middle. On the shell, my mom had painted a tiny beach scene. My mom loved the ocean. She used to set up an easel and canvas on the dunes when it wasn't super busy, and she would paint the Maine coastline for what seemed like hours. Sometimes, if it was warm enough, she would pack a lunch and toys and bring us kids. I remember sitting behind her once, watching her intricately brush the canvas in light blues, greens, and beiges . . . I was in awe. That was the day I acquired my love for painting, especially seascapes.

When I handed Evie the bracelet, she was shocked and asked me where I had found it. I knew that my dad had given her one recently because it was in my mom's will that each of her daughters was to receive a shell bracelet on her eighteenth birthday, and her son got one as well. My dad shared my mom's wishes with me when he gave me my bracelet. At first, I didn't understand since I wasn't Angie or Evie, but he explained to me that my mom had told him to give me a bracelet too so that I could someday gift it to someone who was special to me. I knew that I wanted Cora to have it, and it's fitting that she gets it for her eighteenth birthday as well. I just didn't think we'd be broken up and I wouldn't be the one to give it to her.

I didn't want Evie to know what my mom's wishes were for my bracelet. I knew that if I told Evie the truth, she never would have taken the bracelet or presented it to Cora as her own. I lied and said that our mom had created the bracelets to sell, and when she passed away there was one left behind that I took for myself. She bought the story. All I asked from Evie was that she take a picture of Cora with the bracelet on, so I could see if she liked it or not. Evie called me a creep, and then said she would take a creepy photo for her creepy brother.

The night of the concert, Evie sent me a blurry photo of Cora. She had straightened her hair and it was long, longer than I remembered, and her classic red streaks were faded to a caramel-orange color, or maybe it was just the graininess of the photo? Her head was tipped back with her eyes closed and mouth open like she was singing her heart out to a song. One hand was placed on her chest and the other hand was in the air, fingers splayed wide open and my mom's bracelet clasped around her wrist. She looked like she was reaching for something in the sky.

I wish I had taken the photo.
I wish I were there with her.

CHAPTER SEVENTEEN

Your Song

In the past two weeks, Taylor and I have hung out together nearly every day. We've been so inseparable that she even tags along with my mom and me to yoga twice a week now that the basketball season is over. Taylor and I spend a majority of the class giggling at each other when we fall out of the poses. My mom ignores our antics, but I've caught her smiling at us a couple of times. And Taylor hasn't failed to notice that Lucy has done a total one-eighty. She mentioned that not only does Lucy look happier but she's also nicer . . . and fun to be around. My best friend's not wrong. I have a small inkling that my mom may be dating someone, but I don't want to jump to conclusions. Best to wait for her to tell me if she wants to.

Last weekend, I found out I've been accepted into two community colleges that I applied to last month. At the time, I wasn't sure what I wanted to study, but I've enjoyed photography to the point where I'm no longer taking photos only for class but more for my portfolio or just for fun.

My teacher has told me on multiple occasions that I have a future in photography, and although I enjoy it, I think I'm really interested in marketing and advertising as a career. Kyle helped me with my decision since he's always telling me that "technology is the way of the future." With his dad working in tech, Kyle probably knows what he's talking about.

I've decided that I will major in marketing and advertising, and either minor in photography or just continue to do it as a hobby and see where it goes. Once I knew what I wanted to study—and that I did in fact want to attend college—I asked both of my parents to meet with me at the house to speak to them regarding my future. My mom's been waiting for this discussion for months, and it went well, all things considered. I did most of the talking, and they had enthusiastic responses and gave me sound advice regarding which college to choose. The smiles on their faces warmed my heart, and I was content for the first time in months. I couldn't help but feel as though my dad and I were mending our relationship as we bonded over what was to come.

Today, Taylor is on her way over to pick me up and head to Cal's. The bar is having some weird event called "Calapalooza." Fifteen pop/punk bands are performing back-to-back as a final goodbye to the wonderfully sketchy dive bar. Each band gets forty-five minutes of play time, meaning it's going to be a long freakin' day. They are trying to model the event after Lollapalooza or Warped Tour—hence the cheeseball of a name. I couldn't roll my eyes hard enough when I heard it.

Initially I wasn't planning on going. But after days of Taylor trying relentlessly to convince me, I finally caved—under one strict condition: we make sure not to stick around while The Restrictions perform. Without hesitation, she agreed. Taylor's just excited to be in close proximity to a ton of band boys, she didn't care what my stipulations were.

While getting ready, I tell myself not to put too much thought into my ensemble . . . but I can't shake the thought that I could run into Jeremiah. I won't let myself get too anxious about that possibility, though—I'll try my darndest not to cross paths with him tonight.

I'm wearing my pink Blink-182 cropped T-shirt, along with my white-and-black plaid skirt paired with black tights. Once I finish applying my makeup, I stand back and look at myself in the full-length mirror, my eyes landing on my hair. I hate the way the faded red streaks have grown out, so I make quick work of twisting the strands into a french braid. After I secure the elastic band around the end, I flick the braid behind me so that it rests between my shoulder blades. Smoothing the hair on the top of my head with my hand, I huff a sigh and mutter to myself, "Stop getting your hopes up." Full of conflicting feelings, I force myself out of my room and down the stairs to wait for Taylor.

Sitting at the kitchen island, I hear her horn from the driveway, so I grab my bag, quickly slip on my Vans, and jog out to her car. When I hop in, I look over at Taylor and I can't stop staring at her hair, but also her makeup . . . and her clothes! Her strawberry-blond hair is parted to the side, with her bangs swooped across her forehead to cover most of her right eye. She has dark, thick liner around both eyes and her lids are coated in pink eyeshadow. At first glance, she looks more like a raccoon with an eye infection. She's wearing a tight vest with a black T-shirt underneath, tight black jeans, and a spiky studded belt hangs around her waist.

This is not Taylor's typical look.

"What the fuck are you wearing?" I ask, laughing.

"Shut up, Cora! This is the style," she retorts as her cheeks flush red. But I know Taylor, and she doesn't care what people think, so they won't be red for long.

I shrug my shoulders and shake my head. "If you say so. Own it, girl."

"Fuck yeah, I will," Taylor replies. And with that, she cranks up the music and speeds off to Cal's.

Despite my effort to play it cool, I start to get nervous as we slowly prowl around the parking lot in search of an open spot. Even if we miss The Restrictions' performance, I'm painfully aware that there's still a chance I could run into Jeremiah. I guess I never thought about what I would say or do if I saw him.

I lightly grab Taylor's wrist as her hand grips the steering wheel. "Stop the car, Taylor."

At that exact moment, a parking space appears, and Taylor quickly pulls in and throws the car in park.

"Duh. That's what I'm doing: I'm parking. You have to stop to do it."

"No, Taylor. I can't. Please." My breathing increases and I start panting.

"Cora, what is happening?" Taylor sounds unsettled.

I sit there, taking shallow breaths for a minute before I can get five deep inhales to calm myself down enough to speak.

"I just"—*breath*—"realized"—*breath*—"I might"—*breath*—"have to"—*breath*—"talk to"—*breath*—"Jeremiah."

I fold forward, placing my head between my knees. Taylor leans over and rubs my back.

"Cora, you won't. I already looked at the schedule online and they don't perform until nine o'clock tonight. I texted Chris and he said Miah and Lars had no plans of showing up early."

I lift my head up and look over at Taylor. My heartbeat slows down, and breathing starts to become easier again.

"Oh, thank God," I finally say.

"I'm God," Taylor responds. She giggles and pats my back before jumping out of the driver's side door. She makes her way around the car and opens my door. Taylor offers me a steadying hand and I take it.

"Are you okay, Cora? We don't have to do this."

"I'm much better now. We can do this. I mean, look at you. What a waste of eyeliner this would have been for you if we leave before we even get inside."

Taylor lightly punches my shoulder. "You be quiet. I'm a trendsetter." I link my arm through hers as we begin to walk to the entrance.

"I know you are, BFF."

❊ ❊ ❊

The seventh band of the day just finished performing, and my feet are killing me. My stomach has been growling as loud as the guitars blaring through the amps since the fifth band performed. We arrived at 11:00 a.m. so that we could enjoy the day but leave before any members of The Restrictions show up, but my energy is quickly draining.

I nudge Taylor's elbow and she nods, knowing exactly what I'm thinking. She leads the way out of Cal's, back into the parking lot. We hop into her car to pick up some fast food and chill before we go back in. After scarfing down our meals and listening to Taylor run through all the "hotties" who were looking at us, we decide we are good to watch more bands.

"I have to go pee," I say to Taylor when we get back in.

"Hurry! The next band is amazing—you don't want to miss it."

I glance up at the stage and notice they are setting up a stool and an acoustic guitar. The stage almost looks ready, so I rush off to the bathroom. I make it back to Taylor just as the lights cut off and a single spotlight shines on the stool and guitar in the middle of the stage. We wait for what feels like forever until even the spotlight goes dark and a shadowed figure walks onto the stage, taking a seat and slipping the guitar strap over their shoulder. Everyone looks around in confusion, wondering why there are no lights on.

The strumming of an acoustic guitar begins to hum through an amp and a voice comes through the microphone.

"I wrote this song for you," a familiar voice says, and my heart drops deep into my stomach.

The spotlight comes back on. Sitting perfectly poised on the stool is a guy with jet-black hair with a faded streak of pink down the right side. Miah's face is tipped toward the microphone as he concentrates on the words he's singing. Occasionally his eyes drift to the guitar in his arms, watching his fingers on the fretboard.

I'm in shock. I can't move my body. All I can do is stand and listen to his smooth voice crooning from the speakers. Every word he sings I piece together bit by bit, until I realize he's singing to me. When he reaches the chorus the second time around, he searches the crowd until his topaz eyes land directly on me. His eyes look different, not mysterious but more pained. When he notices that I can't look away, a little grin plays on his lips as he continues to sing. I bite my lip in an attempt to hide my smile.

That's my Jeremiah.

Taylor slides her hand into mine, grabbing my attention. She's smiling at me as she squeezes my hand. I should have known she was up to something, but this... this is perfect.

Jeremiah finishes singing and the crowd claps and cheers, including Taylor. I follow suit and clap loudly. Miah stands up, takes the guitar strap off from over his shoulder, and places the guitar back on its stand next to the stool. He climbs down from the stage and makes his way through the crowd until he's a few feet in front of me. Onlookers are standing around us and I'm becoming self-conscious, but I keep my eyes on Miah. He smirks, but his chin begins to quiver as tears fall from his eyes. I close the gap between us and press my hands to his cheeks, swiping away the tears with my thumbs. I study his eyes, looking deep into that oceanic blue in hopes that I can see what he's thinking, but I don't need to look too hard to know he's sorry. He nods his head in my hands to confirm my thoughts. I wrap my arms around his neck as he wraps his arms around my waist, pulling my body close to his. Holding me as if he never wants to let me go. Our lips meet in an urgent and passionate kiss. All I can think about is how much I've missed the taste of him and his scent that's wrapping around me like another set of arms. I've missed the feel of his body and his warmth against me.

I've missed all of him.

He breaks away from the kiss and looks into my eyes as my heart dives deep down into my stomach for the second time tonight. Gently, against my lips, he whispers, "I'm so sorry, Cora. I love you. I will never comment, like, or look at another girl for as long as I live."

I laugh and shake my head no. "Jeremiah, I should have trusted you. I was such a bitch. I love you so much."

I kiss his lips again.

Miah places his forehead on mine. "I'm so sorry I didn't call or text. I wanted to give you space, but I couldn't wait any longer. I had to tell you I was sorry. I love you, Cora . . . Come on tour with me this summer, please?"

I keep my forehead pressed to his as I feel strands of his hair grazing my temples. For a moment, I almost respond that I can't because my parents won't let me. But I want this, and this is my life.

"Yes. Yes, I want to go with you. I want to be with you."

Miah encircles my waist with his arms and lifts me off the ground. I'm tempted to wrap my legs around him, but I stop myself when I remember that I *had* to wear a skirt today. He holds me close to him while we kiss so hard that my lips start to ache. The sound of cheering and clapping erupts from around us and it startles me. I forgot we had an audience. I can feel my cheeks flush, so I bury my head in between Miah's neck and shoulder. He chuckles and tickles my hip. "What's wrong, Little Jetta? Do you have stage fright?" Feeling the rumble of his laugh through his chest makes my heart swell.

I giggle into his neck. "Miah, that song was beautiful."

He places my feet back on the ground and runs his hand through his hair to push back the pieces that have fallen out of place. "I wrote it for you." He bites the side of his lip as if he's nervous.

"What's wrong, big, mature Miah? Do you have Cora fright?" I tease as I take his hand. He gently jabs his elbow into mine and laughs as he leads me through the crowd toward the exit. I look back over my shoulder to see Taylor. I forgot she was standing next to me while Miah and I were in our own world. Now she's talking to Kyle . . .

When did Kyle get here?

Taylor has her hand on his chest as she laughs. He smirks, watching her like he's infatuated with her. It's all weird, but I don't have time to think about it when I have catching up to do with Miah. I'm just happy Taylor's still having a good time and I'm not leaving her hanging. I want to be a better friend because she's deserving of a great friend.

Miah and I spend the next hour catching up in his car. He fills me in on Angie and how she's feeling good but exceedingly tired. The family is very excited she is having a boy, and her due date is June 27. I thoroughly enjoy watching Miah talk about getting to meet his nephew. He's supposed to be on tour when the baby is born, but he plans on taking the first flight back as soon as Angie is in labor.

I update Miah on the colleges I've been accepted into and what I'm planning on studying, and he's so excited for me.

He tells me multiple times how proud he is of me. I tell him about how my parents are doing and how I've been coming around to the both of them more. Miah asks me if everything is better between Taylor and me, and I let him know she and I had our own falling out but now our friendship is better than ever.

"So why didn't you call or text me?" I suddenly ask Miah.

He rubs the back of his neck, thinking about his answer. "I didn't know what to do. I could ask the same of you..."

I bite my lip in hesitation. "I guess I was embarrassed. I thought we were over for good, and you never wanted to see me again."

"When I hung up the phone with you, I didn't want to break up. I thought we were going to just take some time and this would blow over. But when I didn't hear from you, and you deleted your MySpace... I figured we were over."

I shake my head eagerly. "No, no, never. I felt like our relationship was just getting started, and then I ruined it all."

"Oh shit, wait. Do you have a boyfriend?" Miah asks me in shock. I'm not sure where this is coming from and I don't know how to answer, so I stare at him wide-eyed for several moments.

When I don't respond, Jeremiah speaks again. "When I was grabbing coffee at Grinder's a few weeks back, I saw you with a guy—a good-looking one, I might add."

I burst out laughing when I realize he's talking about Kyle, and I remember how my mom had mentioned that Miah said he saw me with Kyle. Miah watches me laugh, but he has a confused look on his face.

"No. Ew, no. That's Kyle. He's like a little brother to me. We met ages ago at a show and just started hanging out again when we were paired together for a project in our photography class."

"Oh, good. I would feel like an ass if I sat up there singing you a love song and then doing this with you now, all while you had a boyfriend somewhere out there."

I place my hand on Miah's cheek. "There's only one guy for me."

"That's cheesy, but endearing. God, I missed you." Miah leans across the center console and places a kiss on my forehead. I close my eyes and savor this moment. Just the two of us, in the quietness of his car that smells like him, and it feels good. I feel at home and safe again.

I break the silence between us as his lips are still pressed against my head. "Two things, though. One, I'm pretty sure Kyle and Taylor are dating in secret. And two, you need to officially meet my dad now."

Miah leans back into his seat and chuckles. "Okay and okay."

"Oh, and one more thing. I got a job this summer, so we need to talk about tour logistics. I'm broke as a joke."

"Don't worry about the money. I have enough saved for the both of us to survive on tour. Though if you wanted, you could run a merch table for one of the bands and make some cash. We will figure it out. Don't worry."

I could stay in this car with Miah all to myself for the rest of Calapalooza, but eventually we make the short trek back into Cal's so Miah can help The Restrictions set up the stage before they perform. Miah pulls me into an embrace and kisses me before we part ways.

"Wait for me?" Miah asks. He winks at me, and my body responds with goosebumps.

I'd wait a million years for him if he asked me to.

"I'll be here," I reply.

I snake my way through the crowd and find Taylor and Kyle chatting away together. As I approach them, I notice Taylor has her hand placed on Kyle's biceps. Kyle's eyes lock with mine as Taylor turns to see what he's looking at. Her smile and hand drop immediately as her eyes reach mine.

"Sooooo, what's going on over here?" I probe, looking between the two of them.

"Oh, nothing. Kyle was just catching me up on all the stuff you guys have been up to without me," Taylor replies, brushing me off as if she's guilty of something.

I ignore it. Whatever is happening between the two of them, I'm sure they will tell me at some point.

"Taylor, is it cool if I head out with Miah for the night after they perform?" I ask.

"Yes, girl! Go be with your man!" Taylor nearly shouts.

Kyle rolls his eyes and laughs.

The Restrictions play a fantastic set, as usual. When they're done performing, gathering their gear, and packing up the van, Miah and I can finally slip out together. He carefully zooms through the darkened streets back to his place. The entire ride, I fantasize about holding him close again, breathing in the smell of his skin and feeling him inside me. My heart races in anticipation as his car handles the curves like I know he'll handle mine shortly.

Finally, we arrive at his house. Miah leads me up the front

steps, holding my hand as he walks quickly, searching for the house key. As soon as he unlocks the door and we enter the front foyer, he turns and scoops me up again, holding me close to him with his hands on my bum. I wrap my arms around his neck and my legs around his waist, not caring what my skirt reveals in the privacy of Miah's home. Frantically kissing his neck, cheeks, eyelids, forehead, I can't get enough of him. He laughs, and the rumble reverberates through me, sending chills up my spine and making me wet between my thighs.

Miah carries me up the stairs and to his room. He gently lays me on the bed and stands in front of me. I lift myself up onto my elbows.

"God, I've missed you," he says, watching me. He slowly licks his lips, and the motion does not go unnoticed. "I've never felt this way about anyone, Cora. You have your whole life ahead of you, but I'm going to follow you until you tell me you don't want me anymore."

"I want that. I want it all. I love you, Jeremiah Novak," I say as I reach up and grab his shirt, pulling him on top of me.

My heart and mind feel at peace again. I feel *home*.

CHAPTER EIGHTEEN

Pinkies Up

April 2006

Taylor and Kyle are dating. They both realized how much they were into each other at Calapalooza. Kyle asked Taylor out that night and they've been dating ever since. In the past, when I would hang with Taylor and whoever her boyfriend was at the time, I felt like a third wheel. But because Kyle is my best friend too, the three of us have a lot of fun together. It's nice. Taylor seems comfortable with Kyle, like she can be herself. With Lars, although she was happy, it felt like she tried to be too mature and not her usual goofy self. But with Kyle, she's still goofy Taylor.

Jeremiah is meeting my dad tonight. My dad asked if Anne could join us, and I hesitantly agreed. I guess we can kill two birds with one stone: he meets my boyfriend, and I meet his girlfriend . . . or whatever she is to him. I'm not looking forward to it, but Miah keeps reassuring me that it's going to be okay. We decide on a gesture to signal to each other if things get too awkward and we need to bail. Whatever it takes to prevent the night from going down like it did at Loco Cantina. Our gesture is pinkies up while holding our drinks. I couldn't stop laughing at the signal, since we are far from fancy folk.

Miah pulls into the driveway to my house and beeps the horn, right on time. I'm heading toward the door when my mom calls my name. I slip my shoes onto my feet and turn to see her leaning against the wall in the hallway, watching me. She has a smirk on her face, but her eyes are drawn in sorrow. I told her I was meeting Anne tonight. She took the news well, which makes me believe that she is the strongest woman I know.

"Have fun tonight, honey." She pushes off the wall and starts walking toward me.

I'm starting to get nervous, so I shove my hands in my back pockets and fiddle with the hem while I bite my bottom lip.

"I'll try." I laugh nervously and shrug my shoulders.

"I just want to say that I like Jeremiah. He's a good guy," she tells me as she rubs my arm in a reassuring gesture.

"I know you do."

"You are your daddy's little girl, so don't take some of the things he might say tonight too much to heart. I feel like he may be a bit skeptical about your relationship, but Jeremiah will win him over. Don't worry, okay?"

I nod my head yes as she moves in and wraps her arms around my neck, pulling me in for a hug.

"Are you all right with this, Ma?" I ask. My voice is muffled as my face is tucked in between her neck and shoulder.

"Better than you think. Don't worry about me. I know we haven't been separated long, but our marriage has been over for a while. He's happy, and I am too. Truly, I am." She lets go of my neck and stands back. Her warm smile looks genuine now, and I can feel the love and comfort radiating from her.

I do believe she's happy . . . but I know a part of her heart still hurts. I don't know how marriage works, but suddenly not being with someone you've woken up next to for the past twenty years must be heartbreaking. Not that she needs a man to feel fulfilled; I just hope she won't be too lonely or sad tonight.

"Thanks, Mom. I love you." She gently pats my cheeks and turns me toward the door.

"Now go! Prince Charming waits." I laugh at her and open the door as she laughs with me.

When I jump in Miah's car, he turns the music down and leans over to place a kiss on my cheek.

"Hey, Little Jetta, I was beginning to think you were going to be a no-show. Then I'd be stuck having dinner—or breakfast for dinner—with your dad and Anne."

"Oh no, I would never let you go alone," I say with an authoritative tone. Miah just laughs as we begin the drive to the Sea Breeze Diner.

When we pull up to the front of the restaurant, my dad's sitting in our usual booth, the first one next to the door. We never spoke about it being our official booth, but I know my dad prefers it so he can look out the window and at fellow diners as they walk in and out. He enjoys people watching too.

Across from my dad sits a younger woman with long blond hair. Her features are a bit blurry through the window, but I can tell she's younger than my dad by some years. I hadn't realized I was staring until I feel Miah grab my hand on my lap and squeeze it twice. I look down at his hand and then up into his eyes.

"It's going to be okay," he says and then smiles. It's reassuring, and I know Miah and my mom are right. It's just . . . something inside me feels wrong. This feels all wrong. I feel like this chick ruined my family. I mean, no, she didn't. But maybe she did? Maybe she ruined the chance of my parents getting back together and making things work . . . but, maybe she didn't.

I'm so confused. I feel torn. The anxiety is starting to creep into my throat, making it harder to breathe.

"Can I tell you something?" I suddenly ask Miah.

"Yeah, you can tell me anything you want. I would never judge you. You know that."

"I feel like I want to hate Anne, but I also feel like I want to give her a chance."

"I know exactly what you mean, Cece. Hear me out: Why don't you just give her a shot? See what she's like, how she is toward you and your dad. Just see what she's all about. If she sucks, then we bounce. Peace out, Girl Scout."

I start laughing at Miah and my anxiety eases.

"You are so fucking weird," I say.

"You fucking love it," he responds.

Miah gently kisses me on the lips before we both climb out of the car and make our way toward the diner entrance. We slosh through the melting piles of snow in the parking lot. The piles are dirty and I feel like I can relate. I'm going to meet the enemy. Am I betraying my mom? I shake off the thought when Miah holds the door open for me and I slowly enter. When we approach the booth, my dad sees me and slides out.

"There's my little girl!" he exclaims as he embraces me tightly.

"Hey, Dad," I say, my voice a bit shaken from nerves. We break away from the hug and I move back to stand next to Miah again.

"Dad, this is Jeremiah." Miah moves in and places his hand out toward my dad. I notice my dad quickly surveying him up and down, eyes lingering on his tattoos, as he takes Miah's hand into his to return the handshake.

"Mr. Mitchell, nice to see you again," Miah says with a nod.

"Ah, yes. I forgot about our first meeting," my dad replies, standing back and placing his hands in his pockets. He begins clinking his keys as he looks Miah up and down for a second time.

"Well, come sit." He gestures to the booth.

Anne doesn't move as she watches us with a smile on her face.

"Cece, this is Anne. Anne, this is my daughter, Cora, and her friend Jeremiah."

"Boyfriend," I correct him, but he ignores it.

"Oh my gosh, it's so nice to meet you!" Anne says enthusiastically. Her voice is high-pitched and squeaky, like a chipmunk would sound if it could speak.

Standing in front of her, I don't see it. I don't see why my dad would be attracted to her over my mom . . . I guess that's another marriage thing I don't understand. It could also be that I've always thought my mom was beautiful and superior to any other mom or woman in the world.

Anne has dull brown eyes and long blond lifeless hair. It's just straight, no layers or angles, just plain. Her skin is tan as if she frequents the beach a lot, and I feel like she probably does.

It's not all about looks . . . Maybe she's nice?

My dad returns to his side of the booth, and Anne shuffles out to take a seat next to him, leaving Miah and me to make ourselves comfortable across from them. Once settled, Miah takes my hand under the table and holds it for reassurance. I turn and look at him, giving him a gentle smile as if to say thank you.

My dad clears his throat, grabbing our attention.

"Nice to meet you, Anne," I say to be polite.

"I've heard so much about you. You are just so adorable in person," Anne says with a bright, cheerful smile.

With my free hand, I nervously play with a strand of my hair. "Ehh, thanks, I guess."

After the awkwardness of my response, we all sit quietly, picking up the menus lying on the table.

Finally my dad breaks the silence. "So, Jeremiah, what do you fill your days with?" he asks.

We all put down our menus and look to Miah for his response.

"I work for Ava Corp. as their customer service manager. It's a nine-to-five, but when I'm not at the office, I'm either at band practice or performing at a gig. The rest of my time is usually spent with Cora. I also enjoy painting, so I do that too," Miah answers courteously.

"That's great. I hope you aren't taking my girl away from her studies, though. Did she tell you she's going to community college and studying marketing?"

"Yes, she did. I'm so proud of her." Miah looks over at me

and smiles, and I can't help but smile back. It's contagious.

The waitress comes to take our orders and grab our menus. Once she leaves, Miah looks over at Anne. "So, Anne, what do you do?" he asks as he takes the paper wrapper off his straw.

"Well, I used to work as an office manager at Boston Exchange, but I just received my real estate license, so I'll be working for Coastal Real Estate in a week." I can't stop staring at Anne's lips as she speaks. It's as if they move too slow for how fast her words come out. She enjoys overenunciating her words.

"Wow, that's great. Congrats," Miah says.

My dad looks over at Anne and smiles proudly.

"My dad used to be the senior director of finance at Boston Exchange." I can't help it; it just slips out.

"Ahh, that sounds like a great gig as well, Mr. Mitchell."

I don't think Miah noticed I said, "used to." My dad looks over at me. His cheeks are flushed with embarrassment. Anne's face is just as red, and she lowers her eyes to her hands in her lap.

"Yeah, I now work for a start-up company, doing some finance for them. I like it. It's a lot less stressful. Easier work too."

Jeremiah nods his head . . . He doesn't care.

Our food arrives, and we chat about the weather, graduation, photography, and even about Kyle and Taylor.

"Mr. Mitchell—"

"Call me Peter," my dad stops Miah. "You make me sound old calling me 'Mr. Mitchell.'"

Miah laughs. "Peter, has Cora told you about the summer

tour?"

Fuck. No, I didn't, Miah . . . but I guess I am now.

My dad wipes his mouth with his napkin and places it back onto his lap. He squints his eyes at Miah and shakes his head no. "She hasn't. What's the summer tour?"

Miah looks over at me with guilt written all over his face. He realizes I wasn't ready to ask my parents yet.

I quickly jump in on the conversation. "Jeremiah's band is leaving in June to go on tour, and he's asked me to come with him."

My dad's mouth drops open a bit as he stares at me. I know he wants to tell me that I absolutely cannot go on this tour, but he's also thinking he doesn't want to ruin our relationship after we've been getting along so well.

"Oh my gosh! That's so cool! Peter, doesn't that sound like fun?" Anne interjects loudly.

Anne's not too bad.

My dad clears his throat. "I thought you were going to be working at the country club this summer."

Approaching this cautiously, I deliver the response I came up with weeks ago because I knew he'd mention the country club. "Well, I just think this would be a better opportunity for me. I'll get to travel around the country, make friends, have fun before school starts."

"How is that a better opportunity when you don't have two nickels to rub together?" he snaps.

"Actually, Cora is going to sell merch on tour and the bands will pay her," Miah answers on my behalf.

"Well, there you go. Everything's solved," Anne says. She looks over at my dad with flared eyes and a telling smile as if she's saying, "don't do this." My dad looks back at her, shoulders dropping a bit, and I can see he's beginning to back down.

"Yeah, it sounds like you both have it figured out. Just don't forget you have classes when you get back."

"I know, Dad . . . I won't forget," I say in an irritated tone.

We finish dinner, say our goodbyes, and walk back to Jeremiah's car. Miah turns to me as soon as we are in our seats and the doors are closed.

"I'm so sorry, I had no idea you didn't tell your parents about the tour yet," he blurts out as we leave the parking lot.

"No, honestly, it's okay. I was going to have to tell them at some point, and it was nice to have backup," I reassure him.

"I mean, Anne was more backup than I was. She came in clutch," Miah says.

He's not wrong. She did help diffuse the situation.

"Yeah, she did. I guess she's not too bad. I'm not a fan of her voice, but this could work."

"I'm glad we didn't need to use our signal. I was trying to think of a good excuse to bail if we needed to during the tour talk . . . I was coming up short," Miah says with a sigh. But I just giggle as I watch him.

I admire Miah greatly. He's so levelheaded and composed, even in the most stressful situations. I hope I can get to that point in my life someday.

Miah catches me staring, turning my way and then back to the road. "What are you thinking about?"

"Mmmm, just how much I love you and want to be like you." I take his hand that's resting on the stick shift and begin to trace the lines on his palm.

"Why is that?" he asks.

I shrug my shoulders. "You're so considerate, patient, smart, funny, honest... I could keep going all night."

"I'm not always all those things, Cece. I've just learned that it's better to go through life treating others the way that you want to be treated. I don't want to walk around angry, ready for a fight and always having a bone to pick with someone for the rest of my life. Life's too short. I want to be happy. I want to make my time on earth count before I no longer can."

Miah's been through so much in his life. He had to grow up at an early age and figure out life on his own. When his mom passed, he took on the responsibility of running the house, being a parent for his sisters and parenting himself. All while trying to help his dad too.

I admire him for that.

"I think I want to tell my mom about the tour—tonight. In case my dad calls to talk to her about it, I want to be the first to tell her."

"Okay. Sounds good," he responds.

When we arrive at my house, I waste no time breaking the news to my mom. Talking to her about the tour is easier than I thought it would be. She is hesitant at first and asks Miah and me a lot of questions, but then she finally agrees. Her one stipulation for letting me go is that Jeremiah has to promise he will keep me safe and never let me go anywhere alone. My mom didn't need to make that a stipulation; she knows he will take care of me.

After we talk to my mom, Miah comes up to my room to hang out for a bit. He doesn't stick around too long because he has work tomorrow morning and I have school.

I'm so excited that both my parents are allowing me to go with The Restrictions that I can barely sleep. I get to tour the country from Maine to California, which is exciting because I've only ever been to Florida, New Hampshire, Massachusetts, and New York City.

I can't wait to tell Taylor at school tomorrow, but before I drift off to sleep, my eyes pop back open. While I was so amped up about my adventure, I forgot about my last summer with Taylor before college. I don't like the way this feels. I turn on my side and hold my stomach. A slight void forms within me as I think of leaving Taylor for the summer and then rarely seeing her when she's away at college.

I grab my phone from my nightstand and hit Taylor's speed dial number. I don't care that it's 10:30 on a school night, I have to talk to her.

Taylor answers on the second ring. "Cece, my girl. What's up? Aren't you usually in bed by now?" she asks.

"Um yeah, usually. Listen, I have to tell you something."

"Ooooookay. This better not be Kayla McKinnon fucking shit up again."

I laugh. "No, no. Nothing about Kayla."

"Phew, good. So, what's up then?"

"I forgot to tell you at Calapalooza that Miah asked me to go on tour with him."

There's a pause for several seconds.

"Uh-huh," she finally says. "Why is this bad? I'm confused."

"Well, this was our farewell summer before you go to UMaine for the year. We had plans to do all the things we've never done before, and now I won't be here."

"Cora, it's fine. Hey, maybe I can come meet you on tour for a few weeks and we can adventure together?"

The feeling in my stomach subsides.

"That's a great idea! Let's plan it. Wait . . . it won't be weird for you with Lars?" I ask.

"No, not at all. It was amicable, and I've moved on. I'm really happy with Kyle."

"Will Kyle be cool with it?"

Taylor snorts before she answers. "Oh my gosh, yes. He's so easy going, he won't mind at all."

"This is so exciting! I can't wait. This is going to be the best summer ever."

"All right there, old lady, calm down . . . It's way past your bedtime on a school night. I'll see you tomorrow."

I laugh at Taylor's response. "I love you. See you tomorrow."

I still can't sleep after we hang up. My adrenaline is pumping from all the excitement. It's been so long since I've felt this blissfully happy—I can't even remember the last time. I just hope that it lasts.

CHAPTER NINETEEN

Take Care

June 2006

Graduation finally came and went, and it was the quickest day of my life. On top of that, my parents' divorce has been finalized, which happened way faster than I anticipated. I thought for sure I would be packed up and moved out of the house before it was over. But lately fate has had a funny way of dumping major life changes on me all at once.

The graduation ceremony was exactly what I expected, full of cliché pomp and circumstance. To my surprise, I wasn't as happy as I thought I would be. I mean, I was, but sitting in the auditorium and seeing all my classmates hugging and crying made me realize that my life from here on out would never be the same. For the past four years, I had been in a constant routine: get up, go to school, come home, do homework, eat dinner, go to bed, repeat. Now, I don't have a set schedule. I'm free to do what I want. It's liberating, but it also made me sad to know that I won't be seeing the same people every day. After a whole school year of hearing "This is it," it finally makes sense. I guess it's just the comfort of the known. But the moment Kayla McKinnon walked on stage for her valedictorian speech, my sadness was swiftly swept away. On second thought, fuck high school.

My parents showed up and cordially sat next to each other, alongside Jeremiah, Angie, and Evie. When I was called onto the stage, they all cheered loudly and chanted my name. It made me smile, but I was so embarrassed. As soon as I heard them yelling, I put my head down and made a quick exit off the stage. Taylor was laughing at me when I got back to my seat. My face was the same shade as our burgundy graduation gowns, and sweat was dripping down into my eyebrows.

I could never function as a famous person—way too much attention.

Today is the second week of June, and I've spent the day packing for The Restrictions' summer tour. After a long conversation with Jeremiah on the phone last night, I made myself a list of what to pack. Miah told me to keep it light since there won't be a lot of room in the two vans they rented, and the trailer will be full of their band equipment. He also let me know that about 80 percent of the hotels they booked along the way have a washer and dryer. This made my packing list super small but functional. I'm sticking to the basics: T-shirts, jeans, shorts, pajamas, running attire and sneakers, underwear, bras... and the two sets of lingerie Taylor bought me as a "graduation" gift. I wasn't going to pack them, but what the hell. I also threw in the lacy little number Taylor bought me back in February for Valentine's Day. It's purple, so Miah will get a kick out of that.

I've decided to stop packing for the day—I'm pretty much done anyway, and I'm starving. Heading for the kitchen, I pass the window in the hallway upstairs and notice my dad's SUV is in the driveway.

Hmm, that's odd. He rarely ever comes here now . . .

Before I can finish descending the stairs to find out what's going on, I hear my parents arguing in hushed voices in the kitchen. I quietly creep from the hallway to the entryway of the kitchen. Tucking myself behind the doorframe, I stay out of view but am able to glimpse the two of them. I can make out what they are saying, but I have to breathe quietly to hear them.

My dad is whisper-shouting at my mom. "How did you let this happen, Lucy? We had discussed that you were going to tell Cora not to see that boy anymore. What in God's name changed?!"

"Peter, I honestly don't understand what the big deal is. I like Jeremiah, he's a good guy. I trust her with him. Plus, you told me that you didn't mind him."

"Yeah, no, I don't mind him, but I mind that my daughter is with him! She was supposed to be working at the country club this summer. Now she's going to be gallivanting around the country with four boys—hell, men, for Christ's sake! She doesn't have a dime to her name, and what, I'm supposed to fund her adventures? Not happening."

"Well, what does Anne think about this?" my mom snaps back.

I didn't notice how fast my heart had begun to race listening to my dad speak. My blood is boiling listening to him talk about Miah and me like I'm a child, let alone that he's talking to my mom like she's stupid. I have to mentally tell myself to calm down and not do anything rash . . . yet.

"Don't you bring Anne into this. I've already made it very clear that she has no say in what happens in our family."

"Could have fooled me, since she had a say when she hopped into bed with you and ruined our family."

Go, Lucy . . . Though I feel semi-guilty because Anne is nice. But that's beside the point.

"Real nice, Lucy. I can see our daughter gets her maturity from you."

"You know what, Peter? Fuck you. You see Cora twice a month, if that, and you think you can come here and tell me how to raise my daughter? Go to hell!"

My mom turns her back to my dad and continues chopping an onion that's been idly sitting behind her atop a cutting board on the counter. The knife loudly clicks each time it slices through the onion and meets the cutting board. My dad stands with one hand on his hip and the other in his pocket, jingling his keys, as he watches my mom from behind. He has a stern look on his face, like he's ready to tear apart this house, but he stays rooted in place, waiting for my mom to turn back around.

I've got news for you, Peter. I don't think she's going to do what you want her to. Lucy's a new woman.

After several moments, my dad speaks again. "I'm sorry, I honestly don't see the point in her going with him. Furthermore, I just know she will give up on college when she comes back. Do you really want to take care of your daughter with no ambition for the rest of your life? I certainly don't."

I feel tears spring to my eyes. My own father actually thinks I'm a loser with no future, and it hurts something fierce.

My mom slams the knife down on the counter and whips around to face my dad. "God, you are such an asshole, Peter. I'm trying to give our daughter freedom because I trust her. Cora is a *good* girl. She knows what she wants in life, and I'm letting her go get it. You should do the same. I'm done talking about this. Cora is leaving in two days with Jeremiah's band, and we will see her in August. End of discussion." She goes to turn back to the onion, but my dad speaks up and she freezes in place.

"No, Lucy. I get a say in my daughter's life too, and she stays with me this summer."

No, please, Mom. I don't want to live with him. I hate him.

I watch my mom take a deep breath. She starts to walk toward him but stops about six feet away. "That's a shame because that can't happen, Peter. When we finalized the divorce, your affidavit stated that Cora would remain living with me, in this house, until she turned eighteen *and* graduated from high school. So, as far as I can tell, we both don't have a say in what Cora wants to do," she says matter-of-factly.

I'm fuming and about to snap when her words reverberate in my mind.

I'm legally an adult. I don't need them. I can do what I want.

"Oh, that's just great, Lucy. You're being an idiot!" With that, my mom quickly closes the gap between them.

"Get the fuck out of my house. Don't you dare come here and belittle me and make me feel small again. My sister, Karen, was smart to send that letter to your work. You deserved it, and I was too blind to notice how much of a fucking prick you really are. Now, go run back to Anne. I wish her the best of luck." My mom's finger is pointed in my dad's face, and her voice is seething, each word dripping like poison.

I step out from behind the doorframe. My heart is about to explode out of my chest, and I can't bear to listen anymore. My mom and dad look over at me and their faces drop, along with my mom's finger. I don't know what my face looks like, but I imagine it's something like the words my mom just spewed. My nose is flared from how pissed I am having overheard their argument. I stand staring at them both, my hands balled into fists at my sides. My jaw is clenched so tight that I hear it crack from the tension.

"Well, this is awkward . . . Not only were my parents conspiring to break apart my relationship with my boyfriend, but my father also thinks I'm a stupid fucking loser who is going nowhere in life," I grit out through my teeth.

"Cora, it's not—"

"Don't you dare speak," I snap at my dad, cutting him off. His eyes widen as he jerks his head back in surprise.

"For the past few years, I've done nothing but listen to the two of you fight every night, and I endured days on end of you giving each other—and me—the silent treatment. At times, I had to play the mediator just so my own parents would talk to each other. I pushed my life completely aside to be an adult at the age of fifteen. Most teenagers my age were sneaking out of the house, going to parties, getting drunk, and making memories with their friends. But me? ME?! Do you want to know how I spent my nights? Under the covers in my bed, quietly sobbing while I wished that my parents would stop fighting and just love each other again so that we could be happy."

I pause to catch my breath. I'm not even crying because they don't deserve any more of my tears. "You two are pathetic. Mom, not so much. But you, Dad, you are the most pathetic out of any grown-ass man I've ever met. My boyfriend, whom I now know you consider to be some no-good, terrible, low-life scumbag, is more of a man than my own father could ever be. So I'm here to tell you that I'm going on tour with Jeremiah, and until the two of you grow the fuck up, I don't want to see or hear from you again." With that, I swiftly turn and march back up to my room.

"Cora! Cora, honey, please!" I hear my mom begging, but I can't do this anymore. I love my mom and I know she really does want me to enjoy my life and have fun, but I need to get out of here. And that means leaving her behind as well.

I text Taylor on my way up the stairs asking her to come get me. She doesn't even question me, and her reply comes in record time: *Be there in ten.*

While I'm packing the last of my things into my suitcase and grabbing my toiletries off the bed to shove into a bag, my dad enters my room.

"Cora, don't do this," he pleads.

I can't even look at him because I know I can't hold it together. I need to be stronger than that.

"Please, just go away, Dad. Whatever you have left to say isn't going to change my mind about leaving or about you." I jam the toiletry bag into my suitcase. "Mom said it: I graduated and I'm eighteen years old. I can do what I want now." I close the lid of the overstuffed suitcase and try jerking the zipper closed, but it won't budge. With an exasperated huff, I place my body on top of the suitcase to get the zipper to move. I can feel my dad still hovering and watching me as I begin to sweat.

"Cece, let me help you with that—"

Cutting him off again, I spin to face him. "Don't come any closer!"

I turn back to the suitcase and give the zipper one last good yank. The fucking zipper finally glides across and closes the suitcase completely. I chuck the suitcase off the bed and begin rolling it along the floor, heading straight toward the door that my dad just so happens to be blocking, but I don't falter or slow down at all. When he notices, he jumps to the side and knocks over a framed picture. It crashes to the floor. Without turning back to look, I know exactly which picture it is. The photograph is of me, my mom, and my dad at Disney World circa 1996. I was eight and it was our third trip to Disney, but this time was extra special because it was the year I met Belle from *Beauty and the Beast*. My favorite princess. We all looked ridiculously happy in that picture, so I framed it and kept it to remind myself that someday we would get back there again . . . Now, the frame is shattered, just like the three of us.

I wait for Taylor at the end of the driveway with my two suitcases and a backpack. I text Miah to give him a heads-up that I'll be staying at Taylor's the next couple of nights. As I fire off a second message to tell him I'll call him later, my mom appears next to me. Her arms are crossed and she's looking into the distance down the road.

"Cora, I want you to know that I love you. I never wanted to be a part of your dad's plans to separate you and Jeremiah. I understand that you have to do what you feel is right, and I respect that. Just remember while you're out there that I love you. You have been the best gift that life could have ever given me. You are something special."

Almost as if my mom snapped her fingers, my emotions turn from rage and anger to sadness. Guilt riddles me as I think about leaving my mom behind. I do love her very much, and the past six months we've spent together have been some of the happiest moments I've had in a long time. I know she wants me to go on this tour. Her standing beside me right now isn't a ploy to change my mind.

I face my mom, and she follows suit. Her brown eyes are bloodshot, and her cheeks are wet from the tears still dripping down her face.

"Thank you, Mom. I love you so much."

She purses her lips together and her chin quivers as she begins to sob. She reaches her arms out and around my shoulders, pulling me tight to her. We stand at the end of the driveway, locked in each other's arms, sobbing. My mom breaks the embrace and quickly wipes away the tears from my face and runs her hands down my hair, adjusting the strands so they sit perfectly on my shoulders.

"You are so beautiful. Now go, have fun." She spins me around as Taylor's car slowly approaches and comes to a stop in front of us. Taylor hops out of the driver's seat to help me load my suitcases in the back of her Geo Tracker, and I slam the rear door shut.

I climb into the passenger seat, holding my backpack in

my lap. Taylor leans over me to crank my window down. "Hey, Lucy!" she calls to my mom, "I'll take good care of her."

My mom nods and wipes her cheeks and under her eyes to clear away the streaked mascara. "Oh, I know you will," she replies.

As Taylor and I drive away down the street, I can't help but watch my mom in the side mirror, standing with her arms crossed over her chest. She waves, and I wave back out the open window.

Take care of yourself, Mom.

CHAPTER TWENTY

I'll Forgive, but I Can't Forget

July 2012

I step out into the sticky, humid air of a Toronto summer. I lock our apartment door and begin the trek to my favorite café a few blocks away. The sound of horns and sirens is the theme song for my walk. These are the days I wish I owned a car, but Jeremiah convinced me we wouldn't need one living in the middle of the city. He's right... but I miss driving. I miss rolling the windows down and letting the air whip through my hair as the stereo blares my music. Mostly I miss the air conditioning of a car on balmy days like this.

Only four more months...

It helps to repeat my latest mantra. When The Restrictions were on the last leg of their 2006 tour, they were approached by a huge record company based in Toronto and were asked to sign on for a two-year record deal. The band took a couple of weeks to think things over. Each member agreed to the deal, but that also meant they would have to live in Toronto until the album was finished. So the four guys packed up everything from their old Victorian they shared in Portland and headed across the border. Miah had a hard time leaving his family behind, especially his nephew, Colby. The frequent phone calls and texts help, though. It was relatively simple for me to make the move because all my classes were online. I obtained my associate degree in marketing and advertising in the two years the band was under contract in Canada.

The Restrictions finished their album just short of two years after we settled in Toronto. They went on tour shortly after to promote the release of their new album, and the band did amazing. The shows were mostly sold out across the United States and Canada, and they did a handful of concerts in European cities. I couldn't pass up the opportunity to travel around Europe, so I tagged along. It was incredible, and I'm forever thankful to The Restrictions for the experience—and for the thousands of photos I was able to capture.

When we got back from Europe and the tour was finished, Miah and I decided to stay in Toronto since we loved it so much. After touring around with the guys for a few years, I gained valuable experience in the music industry and met a lot of other bands. So in 2010, once I finished my bachelor's degree with a concentration in web design, I launched my career and have been building websites for various musical acts ever since. Just by word of mouth, my clientele skyrocketed, and I found myself becoming overwhelmed. I had an idea to reach out to Kyle and ask if he wanted to help me out and make some cash on the side. He accepted, no questions asked. Kyle graduated with a computer science degree and is a wiz with website design . . . probably better than me, but I'm not telling him that.

Now, after six years, we are finally moving back to Portland, Maine. Our new home is currently being built and construction will be finished in November. We've been traveling back and forth from Toronto to Portland for most major holidays, mainly to visit Miah's family and to be around Colby. As much as we love being on our own in a big city in Canada, living without Jeremiah's family and Taylor and Kyle has been difficult. We just want to be closer to home. Well, his home. My home is wherever Jeremiah is.

The day I left my parents behind was the day I changed my life. I became a happier person, a better person. I've done and tried things I never thought I would in a million years, and it's been thrilling. Some days, I can't believe this is my life. But it's not always easy not being able to pick up the phone and call my parents.

Since leaving Portland, I got a new phone, so my parents haven't been able to reach out to me. They have texted Miah's phone throughout the past six years to say happy birthday and merry Christmas—and they always add, "tell Cora we love her." He does tell me, and I know they do. I've just been waiting for the right time to talk to them again, which happens to be today.

Over the past several years of dating Miah, I learned that relationships are fucking hard. Sure, since I left the drama of high school behind, things have flowed quite seamlessly between us, but it's not always easy. What I've come to realize is that relationships are two people who are continuously growing and evolving within themselves. As they evolve, they must learn how to adapt to the new person their partner is becoming so that the relationship can continue to grow and blossom.

My parents were a couple who were growing individually, but they ended up growing into different people who no longer saw eye to eye. Although I do think that deep down, they both still loved each other in some way, their thoughts and beliefs didn't align in a way that they could make work anymore. My parents didn't handle the separation correctly, but looking back, they just wanted me to have the consistency of two parents in my life . . . but they should have done what was best for them, because it would have been better for me.

Even after all this time, I sometimes mourn the loss of what could have been if all three of us in my family had done things differently. The slight emptiness in my heart hits me at inopportune times, like it did a couple of months after Miah proposed.

We got engaged during our trip back to Portland last Christmas. Miah had booked reservations for us at the old Cal's, which was turned into a swanky steakhouse that Miah "would never go to" (his exact words). I couldn't figure out why he had decided to make reservations there, until after we ate.

The restaurant was all updated on the inside, but the layout was just like the Cal's we remember from the night we met. They had even rebuilt a stage, and a musician was performing with an acoustic guitar. It was a gorgeous night, and the food was incredible. The night ended with Miah popping the question and me saying yes, obviously. But not before I asked, "Are you fucking kidding me?!" I was so surprised . . . I had no idea it was coming.

When everyone in the restaurant applauded, I looked around and noticed Jeremiah's family, his bandmates, and our friends, including Taylor and Kyle, were standing around us clapping and cheering. Miah had rented out the restaurant for the rest of the night and had invited everyone to celebrate with an engagement party right then and there. We all drank and ate more food and partied together. A bunch of us even took turns at karaoke. The singing was wonderfully awful, and it was a night I will never forget.

Blissfully happy with my fiancé, I hadn't noticed anything was missing in my life until it came to me while I was sitting in our apartment by myself, quietly constructing a website for a client this past spring. I kept feeling a nagging in my chest and finally identified it as sadness, but I had no reason to be sad. I couldn't put my finger on where it was stemming from . . . until it hit me. It hit me how badly I wanted to pick up the phone and call my mom to tell her I was engaged. I wanted to listen to her squeal with excitement and call Miah "Prince Charming" again like she used to. I wanted my mom to go with me to find a wedding dress. I wanted my mom to help me pick out flowers and scrutinize reception venues and do all the fun things. I wondered who would walk me down the aisle, even though I wished it would be my dad. But I couldn't have that. I sat with my sadness and asked myself, "Why can't I have that?" The answer was simple: I could.

In realizing all this, I wanted to reach out to my parents and make amends. I had healed my wounds, and it was time to move on from the people we used to be and the mistakes we made in the past. I asked Miah for their numbers and texted them, asking to meet me here in Toronto. They both agreed. Now, on this hotter-than-Hades day, I'm on my way to meet them at my favorite café, Café Paramour. Ironic, I know.

As I'm crossing the street to the café, my nerves start to get the better of me. I've been trying to suppress my anxiety about this day for a while, but now I can't seem to keep it buried. My mind is racing, and I suddenly feel a panic attack coming on. I haven't had a panic attack since I was in high school, and now, at the worst possible time, I'm about to have one. When I've finished crossing the street, I stand in front of the café door for several moments battling with myself if I should go in or bail on this whole thing and go home and tell them I am sick and had to cancel.

This was a bad idea.

What if they hate me? What if they hate Miah? What if we get into a huge blowout in the middle of the café?

I snap out of it enough to pull my phone out of my back pocket. I unlock the screen and call Miah. I don't know when I started pacing up and down the sidewalk, but now I'm chewing my thumbnail as I wait for him to answer.

Miah sounds concerned when he picks up. "Cece, is everything all right? You're supposed to be with your parents."

"I can't do this. I can't go in there, Jeremiah. This was a mistake. I can't—"

Miah cuts me off before I can rattle off any excuses. "Cora, it's okay. Take your five deep breaths. You are okay."

I close my eyes and lean my head back, still holding my phone to my ear. I take five deep breaths, and my heart rate slows back down.

"I know you love your parents, and you want them back in your life . . . They want the same thing, Cora, or they wouldn't have agreed to meet with you. It's going to be okay, and if it's not, then you come home, crack open a pint of ice cream, and we can watch *Twilight*."

I chuckle at Miah's response. He knows me too well. Ice cream and *Twilight* are my guilty pleasures—I don't feel so guilty about the ice cream, but definitely *Twilight*.

"I love you. Thank you," I say, now feeling more relaxed.

"I love you, too. It's going to be okay. I'll be home right after dinner with Mark."

I tap the red button on the screen to end the call and slide my phone into my back pocket once more. I walk up to the door of the café again, but this time I pull it open without letting myself overthink anything.

When I step inside, the arctic blast from the air conditioning hits my bare arms and legs, raising goosebumps all over my body. The smell of rich coffee and sweet pastries envelopes me, and it eases my nerves because it's a sense of comfort. I look around, but I realize that I don't exactly know what my parents look like anymore . . . but I should recognize them, right? They are my parents, after all.

After scanning the café, I spot my dad. I notice his dark hair is buzzed but with small spikes where it's slightly longer in the front, which is a different style from the last time I saw him. His brown eyes are perfectly outlined by dark-brown glasses, another new feature I have never seen. The wrinkles on the side of his eyes from years of dad jokes and smiling with pride and telling funny stories were not as creased as they once had been. But the frown lines around his mouth are deeply embedded in his skin, as if he hasn't laughed or smiled in some time.

My dad is talking to my mom when he looks up and notices me. My mom's sitting across from my dad. When she notices he's no longer looking at her nor speaking, she whips her head around and her eyes meet mine. Still standing at the entrance, I watch my mom immediately shoot her chair out from behind her legs and rush toward me. Approaching me with her arms outstretched, she stops a few inches away. I haven't moved. Both of my hands are gripping the strap of the purse hanging on my shoulder. My eyes brim with tears, but I try unsuccessfully to blink them back. I can't fight the sting, and those damn tears begin to roll down my cheeks.

I can't remember the last time I cried.

Without any more hesitation, my mom wraps her arms around me in a loving embrace. Her hug is tight, as if she's afraid that I'll turn and walk away like I did six years ago.

"I love you . . . I've missed you . . . You are so beautiful," she whispers into my hair over and over again. A rush of her perfume comes over me. I hadn't noticed how she always wore the same perfume all those years back. I was so used to smelling it every day. But now I'm remembering the small details I had forgotten about my parents. The small details that meant nothing back then, but they mean something now.

As we pull back from each other, my mom presses her palms to my cheeks. Her eyes roam around my face as she smiles, but her smile has pain behind it. I look back at her perfectly tan face, with her light makeup, silver eyeshadow, and soft brown eyes that have aged since I saw her last. My heart begins to break thinking of all the years we lost.

My mom steps aside and my dad is now standing a few feet from us. A lump forms in my throat when I see him waiting there. I remember the things I said to him and the things he said about me all those years ago. It hurts, but it's also embarrassing to think I was so young and naïve. His excuse isn't the same as mine, though.

I move a step closer toward him. Somehow, and for some reason, I manage to croak out, "I'm so sorry."

My dad places his hands on my shoulders and intensely looks into my eyes. It makes me feel a bit uncomfortable, but this whole thing is uncomfortable for me. His face slowly starts to turn red, which is soon followed by him choking back tears as he shakily pushes the words out. "No, I'm sorry. I was such a terrible person back then. I don't even know who I was."

After those words are spoken, that's when I close the small gap between us and embrace him. I wrap both my arms around my dad's torso. It was the only place I could ever reach to hug him when I was younger, unless he picked me up and held me.

We take our seats at the table my parents had already claimed before I walked in. My mom and dad are sitting next to each other, and I claim a chair across from them. We each order a coffee, and I get a sticky bun for the table. They are the best sticky buns in the city—in my humble opinion—and they are about the size of my head and topped in a gooey brown sugar glaze with little bits of perfectly toasted chopped pecans. When the barista brings over our order, I see my parents' eyes widen at the sight of the sticky bun.

I can't help but laugh. Jeremiah's expression was the same when I first got one for the two of us.

"It may look large but don't worry, we will finish it. It's like eating super tasty air, it's so light and fluffy but *so good*."

I smile and grab a fork to dig in, and my parents follow my lead. They each take a forkful and in unison all we can say is "Mmmmmmmm." My smile grows wider as I watch my parents nod their heads as they chew.

"Oh my, you were not wrong," my mom gushes. Her hand is covering her mouth since she still has a bit left to chew.

"No, she was not," my dad agrees.

For the next two hours, we sit and sip our coffees, catching up on the past few years. Most of the conversation consists of my parents peppering me with questions about my life here with Jeremiah. We briefly chat about the past, but it's a very short conversation. My dad asks me what I'm doing for work now, so I fill them both in on how I attended college online and earned my bachelor's degree. I tell them all about the bands I've met and how I toured around Europe with The Restrictions. I show them some of the photos I have on my phone, and they love it. My dad makes a comment that stands out to me, about how Jeremiah has done well for himself. It's true, he has. I'm proud of Miah, and I don't tell him enough.

I also show my parents some of the websites I've created, and when my mom compliments the photographs on one of the sites, I blush. Shyly, I respond to her comment. "Those are mine too."

When I look up at my mom, her mouth is wide open as she swats my dad's arm to get his attention. "Peter, you *have* to see these." Then to me, she says, "Show your dad, honey."

I hand over my phone to my dad and I nervously watch him as he pinches the screen to zoom in and out.

"Cora, you are really something else. Those are very cool," he says as he hands my phone back to my mom.

"She definitely gets her creativity from me," my mom says, nodding her head.

"Whatever you say, Lucy," my dad responds in a teasing tone.

My dad glances at his watch and then at my mom. "Hate to do this, kiddo, but your mother and I have a plane to catch in a couple of hours, so we should make our way to the airport."

"How long were you both in town for?"

"We flew in yesterday morning, and we fly out tonight. A quick trip," my mom replies.

"Yeah, very quick." The tinge of sadness in my voice surprises me.

"Well, we've been waiting to see our girl for a long time; we couldn't pass this up. With you moving back, though, we hope we can see you more." My dad is twisting his empty paper cup in his hands as he talks.

I want to hear more about their lives. We were so busy talking about Miah and me that we don't have much time left to talk about them. "When Miah and I move back in November, would you both like to come to dinner at our place?" I ask hesitantly. "I feel as though you know all about my life, but I would really like to hear about your lives. Plus, I know Miah would love to have you both over."

"I would love that. Just text me a date and time, and I will be there," my dad answers. He partially turns to my mom but is looking between us both when he asks, "Would you mind if I brought Anne along?"

He looks ashamed for mentioning her name, but I'm just proud of him for asking.

I shift my gaze to my mom to gauge her response. She simply nods at us both.

"Sure, that would be fine," I say.

"I would love to come. I too would like to bring someone, if that's all right. His name is William," my mom says.

A smile spreads across my face, stretching from ear to ear. I'm relieved that my mom hasn't been alone all these years. She looks great too. I have to remind myself to thank William when I meet him, for giving my mom that "glow" I can see all around her. She looks like the beautiful mom I always admired and aspired to be when I was a little girl.

The three of us say our goodbyes before heading in opposite directions outside the café. My dad hugs me once and then again, all while telling me how proud of me he is. My mom gives me one very long hug, and we silently hold each other.

When we part, I get about four steps down the sidewalk when I hear my dad's voice calling out to me.

"Cece, WAIT!"

I turn and do as he says while he jogs toward me.

"I forgot to ask you to do something for me." He's catching his breath, so I give him time. "Could you please tell Jeremiah I said thank you? Thank you for taking care of my daughter when I should have, and thank you for believing in her when I should have."

Without answering him, I lunge forward and wrap my

arms around his waist, resting my head against his chest.

"I love you, Dad," I say, though it's barely audible.

"I love you too, my little girl." My dad's voice cracks, and I can hear him sniffling, but I don't want to move. There's too much comfort in his embrace, and I missed him.

After relishing my dad's hug, we finally let go of each other if for no other reason than he has a plane to catch. I watch him walk back to my mom, still kind of amazed at how far we've all come since the last time we spoke.

When I arrive home from the café, Miah is still out grabbing dinner with his band manager, Mark, so I decide to make some progress on one of the websites I am redesigning. I sit at my computer, just staring at it, as my mind drifts off to thoughts of my childhood and my parents. I replay our meeting at the café over again in my head, and I really home in on how I am feeling: there is a calmness inside me now, and I began to feel it as I was walking home tonight.

I feel at peace. I feel complete.

* * *

Jeremiah comes in later that night. I am already lying in bed, but not asleep. I hear him shuffling around the bedroom, so I roll over and flick on the bedside light. I'm surprised to see him sitting in the chair across from the bed, wearing nothing but his black boxers. His tan acoustic guitar is strapped around him and he begins to strum slowly back and forth across the strings. He stops to look up at me and smiles. Before I can ask him what he's doing, he places his pointer finger to his lips. So I swallow back my words and sit all the way up to watch what he will do next. Miah begins playing again, and it's a tune I'm very familiar with . . . it's my song. The song he wrote for me and performed at Calapalooza. Sometimes, when I'm having trouble sleeping, Miah will sing me my song.

I sit in bed and watch him quietly sing and strum the guitar. I can't help but smile as my heart flips around in my chest at the sound of his voice and the way the muscles in his arms flex.

Good god, he's so hot.

Miah finishes the song, and before I can demand that he join me under the covers, he rises from the chair and puts the guitar back on the stand. Then he's on the bed, crawling toward me until he is overtop of me, face to face.

With a dip of his head, he whispers onto my lips, "I love you, Cora Novak."

"I'm not your wife yet." I laugh, working my hands through the back of his hair. "Hey, Miah, can you promise me that we will always stay like this?"

Miah softly kisses me, and my eyes flutter closed. When I no longer feel his lips on mine, I open my eyes to find his topaz-blue ones looking directly into mine.

When he speaks next, his tone is soft and velvety with an underlining tone of seriousness as he says, "Little Jetta, I'll stay any way you want me to for as long as I'm alive."

Me too, Pinky.

The End

JEREMIAH'S SONG TO CORA

Verse 1
Your eyes are shining and brightening my core
There's nowhere else I want to look now
Just one glance and I promise that from now on I'll go wherever you want to
If you tell me to stay, I'll wait right here for you every day

Chorus
So let's forget the world outside and what was in our pasts
Let's take this world by storm
Don't worry about our age gap as our walls begin to crash
Whatever we want, we can have
Because I love you like no one ever has

Verse 2
I'll keep your heart and mind from harm's way
Since Earth can be such a dark place
I won't let this shit take away your smile
Your laugh is on repeat in my mind, and it's my favorite melody

Bridge
This is the first day of our lives,
Keep thinking someday I want to make you my wife
But you have so much life to live, and who am I to stand in your way?

Chorus
So let's forget the world outside and what was in our pasts
Let's take this world by storm

Don't worry about our age gap as our walls begin to crash
Whatever we want, we can have
Because I love you like no one ever has

Verse 3
I can't wait to see the woman you become
I know you'll create masterpieces and stand for what is right
You'll radiate and people will bask in your light
I will stand for what is right too as I stand behind you
I'll be with you until you tell me enough

Chorus
So let's forget the world outside and what was in our pasts
Let's take this world by storm
Don't worry about our age gap as our walls begin to crash
Whatever we want, we can have
Because I love you like no one ever has

ABOUT THE AUTHOR

Kristie Price

The Restrictions of Cora is Kristie's debut novel – and it will not be her last.

Kristie spends most of her time reading (shocker!), chasing two toddlers around, cuddling with her two golden retrievers, and diving deep into romance and mystery-binge-worthy shows.

When Kristie's not reading, mom'ing, and solving mysteries – you can find her meditating (when her best ideas come to her), attending concerts, being in nature, and baking.